# In the Country
# of the Blind

Center Point
Large Print

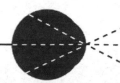

**This Large Print Book carries the
Seal of Approval of N.A.V.H.**

# In the Country of the Blind

## Edward Hoagland

CENTER POINT LARGE PRINT
THORNDIKE, MAINE

This Center Point Large Print edition
is published in the year 2017 by arrangement with
Skyhorse Publishing.

The text of this Large Print edition is unabridged.
In other aspects, this book may vary
from the original edition.
Printed in the United States of America
on permanent paper.
Set in 16-point Times New Roman type.

ISBN: 978-1-68324-327-4

Library of Congress Cataloging-in-Publication Data

Names: Hoagland, Edward, author.
Title: In the country of the blind / Edward Hoagland.
Description: Center Point Large Print edition. | Thorndike, Maine :
Center Point Large Print, 2017.
Identifiers: LCCN 2017000935 | ISBN 9781683243274
    (hardcover : alk. paper)
Subjects: LCSH: Large type books.
Classification: LCC PS3558.O334 I5 2017 | DDC 813/.54—dc23
LC record available at https://lccn.loc.gov/2017000935

For Mary and Molly

# In the Country of the Blind

# Chapter 1

Carol's fluctuating needs or whims occupied more than their fair share of his thoughts, since her visits were irregular, but on the other hand, she claimed she thought of him too. "Fugitive thoughts," he labeled them, although of course they were a lifeline of a sort. What would his children discover of him in closets or wherever? Would Claire scrub all remnants of him out of the house, bundle his clothes into cardboard boxes for the thrift shop, throw out even the briefcases he'd emptied his desk drawers into? They didn't just contain tax receipts, but jottings of the personal kind that could give a grandson or daughter inklings about an absent parent to stir affection and nostalgia. He'd left them there because, although he couldn't read anymore, he didn't want to hire strangers to read these private musings to him later on, and he couldn't bear to simply pitch them out yet either. Maybe Molly or Jeremy someday would be the ones to discover, retrieve, maybe even read them to him in old age. He trusted that his better nature was recorded there, not doggerel or folderol, but would Claire by and by throw them out? His own father's papers had disappeared during his mother's widowhood—also his grandfather's World War I uniform—and she'd been grieving for him, not feeling guilty like Claire, or angry. What did you give your kids, besides a lottery of genes? A stance—that mix of bluff and confidence, backbone and wussiness that passes for personality or character. One talks less about ethics after third grade. Don't steal candy or hit other children, if they hadn't learned the costs of violence on their own. Press transposed himself to half-imagined school settings, buildings he remembered at least, although the teachers would have changed. And Claire too; her harried routine was the politics of her job in marketing, which was more fluid than his had been at Merrill Lynch. He had no idea how her new relationship was going, but found he wished her well. Fatalism about his fading eyesight produced more generosity than bitterness he found.

Survival seemed the watchword at first, but that had proved a given when you had money trickling into the local bank from a trust he had created to live on. On either side his neighbors, the Swinnertons and the Clarks, watched out for him, the former in particular because he had bought the old Swinnerton farmhouse and much of the property that went with it and biked over for hearty lunches, farm-style, at the house they lived in now, for five dollars a day or so, and company. Karl Swinnerton was a woodsman, content to see his father's dairy herd sold off, except for a relic

Jersey in Press's barn, with a Percheron that hauled logs, and banty hens nesting in the hayloft. Fiftyish and living a few miles south of Canada in uppermost Vermont, Karl had never been to the cities, but knew city men from training their duck dogs in Ten Mile Swamp, which stretched below the downhill pasture, or else guiding them in deer season, grouse season, bear season, or traveling to field trials where setters he'd trained competed, pointing at game-farm pheasants placed in the brush to shoot. A World War II veteran, he was good with guns and a Legion stalwart but not a gun nut, and believed, like Press, that Richard Nixon was letting the Vietnam mess drag on too long. Press had been a customer's man at the brokerage firm before losing his sight, but Karl believed in private enterprise, so they'd found little to argue about at lunch. Anyway, Karl's radio scanner was always on because he was Athol's volunteer fire chief, so they heard every ambulance call and police bulletin; even the nearest railroad dispatcher and airport control tower, not to mention sheriff's natter. Karl had seen action at Anzio in Italy and combat at the Colmar Pocket in France, on a continent he never wanted to return to, so he judged a man not by surface geography, like birthplace, education, money, but how he might hold up during a fire or in a firefight. Thus Press, though an unknown quantity, pleased him by grittily riding a bicycle over for lunch on a road he couldn't see, but felt the gravel along the shoulder crunch under his wheels and navigated by the telephone poles intermittently alongside, quite topsy-tilty on his retinas.

Dorothy Swinnerton, by contrast, had been to Boston and New York even as a child with her brothers, selling a truckload of Christmas trees on the sidewalk to passersby. They'd sleep in the cab that night, but Dorothy was sometimes invited to stay in the apartment of one of her family's summer boarders, city spinsters of both sexes who paid to spend a couple of weeks in the fresh air on their front porch, eating homemade cottage cheese and berry pies, eggs they collected themselves warm from the henhouse, nervous folks with tics and allergies and phobias, to escape the vise of city life. She'd hung about them in July and August while growing up and in her teens sold raw milk, cream, maple syrup, basswood honey, and pies to summer people around the lake from a horse-drawn wagon, getting to know a wide assortment of relatively sophisticated or metro-politan characters, almost like going to college, she thought. They read books and magazines, questioned her gently but intelligently, maybe even suggesting she show them poems or school papers she'd written, which turned out to seem important in retrospect when she began writing for the women's page of the local paper— successful partly because her viewpoint was sympathetic to and informed by seasonal visitors too. So she took Press under her wing matter-of-factly, careful to display no pity, just friendliness and tolerance.

The Clarks were a different kettle of fish. Evangelicals, they took Press to church with them as well as to the supermarket. In the pews he was hugged comfortably by everybody, invited to Sunday luncheons after the service by strangers whose faces he couldn't see, and then driven home by them after possibly being asked a little about mortgages or such, but nothing to argue about apart from Evolution. The congregation supported a mission in Africa, but charity of course begins at home. The Clarks, Darryl and Avis, liked farming and milked sixty cows, twice a day, three-hundred-sixty-five days a year and grew the corn and hay that fed them. Karl called them "Christers," but Dorothy respected them and confided that people had doubted she should marry into the Swinnerton clan because Karl's father was known for cooking moonshine and brewing and selling bathtub beer right on the place, and his granddad had run rum from Canada through Ten Mile Swamp during Prohibition, once shooting a revenuer, people said. Karl was a pillar of the town as fire chief and Legion commander, but his dad, besides bootlegging, had contro-versially employed jailbird crews in his logging operations down in the swamp, renting them from the county or the state. This meant familiarizing a further criminal element with the trails down there, leading into Canada, now used not for whiskey but by people-smugglers. Karl himself— though a fireman, not a lawman, by his own description, preserving that much family loyalty— had recently found a dead "Chinaman" on one of the paths, he told Press and Dorothy. Buried him decently but didn't report it. Not that the sheriff would especially want to know, and he didn't care for the Border Patrol. But it preyed on Karl's mind.

"You don't know he was from China. The poor fellow. He might have been Vietnamese or from Thailand," Dorothy pointed out, arguing with the term but not suggesting the Feds should have been notified. There was enough hubbub on the road anyhow, what with hippies coming in to join the commune up the hill and doubtless planting pot. She was afraid one of them was going to hit Press on his bike, they drove so fast. But she'd contributed a scarf with an Oriental motif for the burial of the unfortunate victim Karl, working alone, had performed. It was pitiful to think of him shot maybe for giving his smugglers some lip. She had to bite her tongue not to write a column about it for the *Weekly Chronicle*. The editor turned down plenty of her ideas, but surely this would float. Last week, for example, she'd wanted to explore the rumor that the hippie women at the commune were gardening bare-breasted to "help the veggies grow." Benny, the junkyard owner, adjoining the Swinnertons on the other side, had unlimbered his telescope, yet both Karl and the editor had said no. Her last piece had been about the moccasin-flower orchids in the swamp that savvy families used to pick for their daughters' senior prom. Karl had helped with that, as well as another on how to catch snapping turtles and cook them into savory stews. Her most popular this year had been "Explaining Summer People," which was funny yet so respectful to everybody that nobody was mad.

Dodging the bullet of loneliness this way and that, Press listened to the regulars morning and evening on the radio, including French DJs emanating from Quebec, conversed at normal voice with himself, his absent children and friends, and listened to the aviary of songs and sounds outside: owls, finches, loons, and wrens; a buddy having mailed him a bird tape. To lose one of your senses was a test of character. Could you grow a new limb? He felt undressed sometimes, semi-blind, as if he'd left off his shirt or pants. Though he didn't understand French, he tuned in a certain female classical music host every day for her comforting, wifely but seductive voice. A smart parishioner at the Clark's Solid Rock Gospel Church loaned him a sizeable sundial to read on good days instead of deciphering his

15

clock. His ears, nose, and sense of touch felt alert to duties enhanced. Feeling the windchill, he gazed into the sky for a forecast, triangulating by the wind. He could hear rain and smell humidity. The big barn's shape, the house, and shade trees were visible, along with the overgrown log truck track leading down from his drive into a cedar and tamarack forest bordering the swamp. For exercise he liked to descend and wend back up, careful not to stray onto a game trail or side path, where he'd get lost. The wood thrush calls around his house were a beacon, like the meadow's pale green, where a friend of Karl's still grazed heifers, the mountain's bulk rising gradually across the paved road. White birch trees beckoned there, among the beech and maple. The spring which fed his plumbing was located there and Benny Messer, the bearlike junkyard man, had submerged himself in it to clean out the silt and broken tiles and a boulder that had fallen in. Press traced the backhoe path over the new pipe Benny had laid, though the tumbly, noisy stream paralleling it nearby was more intriguing—with its pools underneath mini-waterfalls, amber sands, and rooster combs of clashing current he admired while laying his cheek against the moss.

Press kept scrambling upwards, alongside, to explore the creek, and how could you get lost; just follow it down. But one day a tiff between his benefactors, the Clarks and Swinnertons, soured his mood. That is, listening to it, which didn't merely involve Bible-believing versus free-thinking, but a Swinnerton son, now grown and gone. In the Clarks' minds he had done their only daughter wrong. Shifting back and forth between the kindly households got somewhat claustrophobic. And Karl was developing emphysema or something that worried Dorothy and left him breathless on fire calls. Financially worried also, not eligible yet for Medicare, they had preoccupations at property tax time. Heat from the woodstove was free, and milk, eggs, and garden produce, not to mention the wild meat and fish he shot or caught, but living cashless was increasingly uneasy. No monthly milk check from the wholesaler, no boarder or baking income except for Press, hound and bird-dog training petering out as Karl lost interest in catering to the clientele. For Karl, Press was a client, for Dorothy a chum, for the Clarks a project, and he was grateful for his luck in neighbors, but the daily hammer of his handicap needed more of an outlet. On the phone he was exhausting the free time of his old friends, even long-lost ones, who might suspect he was angling for an invitation to be taken in.

Impulsively, therefore, he pushed on upstream one afternoon after a gloomy lunch at Karl's, who'd been complaining that the new loan officer at the bank, for the first time, was a woman, who was also the branch manager. Talking to a woman you barely knew about urgent personal needs bothered him, though in principle he said he didn't oppose women's rights. So, lonely-ish, with the white birch bark beckoning and a winter wren's intricately repeated call, Press grabbed outcroppings and windfalls along the water's way, careful not to twist an ankle. But he'd kept his body shipshape, was not winded or at a loss for where to go—just stay next to the dry side of the bed the rustling stream had carved for itself.

It popped, plopped, silkenly rushed, or raucously collided with subsided rocks and boulders and fallen trees. He could see the pewtery, silvery, greeny, amber, or foamy white colorations also, reflecting the trunks and crowns of a forest so mature that he could see its shapes. Even a diving frog or twirling trout registered, and the blue sky. Stepping stones choreographed his ascent as well as the water's hop yard by yard down toward the swamp, past soft leaf beds under smooth-skinned beech, fragrant basswood, then spiky spruce and pine. After resting on a cushion of moss he scrambled on until a particularly inviting pothole struck him as deep and placid as a bubbly bathtub, under what sounded like a sort of ladder of little falls. He was tempted to stop and skinny-dip before perhaps turning back, but was startled to hear a woman's angry shout from above, not just that he was beginning to take his clothes off but was here at all.

"Keep away from him! Who is he? Why is he here? Get out of here!"

Press realized the woman might be speaking to her children, so trod cautiously, buttoning his shirt again and waiting to answer her by announcing he was blind, as it occurred to him that she might be bathing herself. Kids were approaching, remarking to each other that no, they didn't recognize him—who was he? Turning to their voices, he said his name and "How are you? Any place to swim?"

A boy and girl, they didn't answer, but shortly shouted uphill, "Mom, he's blind!"

She sounded incredulous, torn between extreme suspicion and wanting to react as if to an automobile accident. "Bring him up here," she said; then countermanded herself, maybe remembered hearing about a blind man living on Ten Mile Road. "Are you lost?"

"No. Just exploring," he explained in an ordinary tone to allay her fears, and as she waved her hands in front of his eyes when she got near.

"How are you going to go home? I'll take you home," she suggested.

In his loneliness, Press didn't simply introduce himself but a capsule of his life's situation. And Carol gingerly let down her guard, taking his arm to help him to her car. The kids interrupted, taking his hands to have the fun of leading him; then complained they hadn't gotten in their wash or swim. "The Tubs" was the name of this stretch of creek and since their cabin had no hot water, they indicated, this was better than a sponge bath out of a pail at home. Press offered to sit down somewhere while they did that, and everybody joked about whether he was "blind enough" to be allowed to "watch." Carol asked for more details of his condition.

The trio did skip back to Jack Brook to finish their ablutions while he waited thoughtfully on a log. When they were through and she had confidently grasped his arm again, Carol (he liked the name) asked whether he'd ever read "Hansel and Gretel"—whose witch would have thrust him straight into her oven after she lured him into her hut in the woods.

"Little did you know!" she exclaimed. "But I'm an artist. I won't. I'll render you in another way."

He could distinguish the outline of her log cabin with a car in front and hoped to be ushered in. She told him water for her sink ran winter and summer through a hose from the brook, cold enough for a cooler and drinkable. But she put him in the car instead and drove him back to his house, coming inside to "case the joint." The kids had stayed on the mountain, "Though they'd love it," she said, tramping upstairs and down; a ladder led to the attic.

She opened the refrigerator. "So you have food." And switched the lights on and off, laughing because he didn't need any, whereas they, living off the grid, had none. She wouldn't stay and brew tea, as he suggested, but told him again, "I'm an artist. You worked with money. So I want you to sculpt me in your mind's eye, like for practice." Then rather than hug him politely good-bye, she took his hand and cupped it over her breast. "Remember. Sculpt me," she said again—"Be an artist," before driving off.

That night he did what Onan did, if that properly counted, and tried to remember if Carol had ever divulged her last name, so he could try Information. But since she lived without electrification, presumably she had no phone line either. Nor had he seen the route by dirt road to where she lived, or her face and clothing in detail. Her kind clutch on his arm while steering him from what she called Jack's Brook to her cabin was incrasable however as a memory, and her hair, long enough to swing as they walked and touch him occasionally too. Was she a hippie? He knew the term, of course, but his sight had dimmed before they became omnipresent, at least in the quarters he'd frequented, suburban Connecticut, uptown New York. Even the Clarks and Swinnertons knew next to nothing about the nearby commune, only the farm family who'd sold them their land—which Karl had hunted and trapped on since boyhood until now. Benny, the junkyard man with the telescope, who wrestled the boulders out of Press's spring-hole, was the only one who'd been up their drive, because the men bought car parts from him. Their barn had been carpentered into apartments, he claimed, and the farmhouse resembled The Old Woman's Who Lived in a Shoe and had so many children she didn't know what to do. The school bus driver thought so too. Yet they had phones and electricity, while Carol's was like another century—or maybe an artist's retreat, since that's what she said she was.

She seemed to want him where she wanted him, if she wanted him pining for her; Karl and Dorothy could shed no light on the mystery of Carol's identity, or which hippie was which, and their warren of bungalows and huts. "Don't get into drugs," Karl warned tersely. "They have their own trails into Canada, Benny thinks, over the mountain." Obviously nobody was tipping off the Feds, and it was not like people-smuggling through the swamp. More highbrow? as Press joked to himself, so many hippies supposedly were college grads.

Carol did show up, kids in tow, three days later. "Did I see hamburger in your freezer? If you're not busy, we came to mooch." They were already exploring; she must have told them about the attic ladder and a tire hanging from the maple bough in back.

"What do you look like?" he asked. "I've been trying to imagine." They both laughed.

"You mean you won't feed us if I'm not good-looking? Next time, if you're good, I might cook for you. In fact I'll do it now—stay away from that stove—after my bath. And no, you can't watch. But since you *can't* watch, you can keep me company," she added.

"For my sculpture?"

They laughed again. She told him she worked in stained glass, like her father, a church-window creator.

It seemed so improbable for an apparently hippie woman to have a father doing Virgin Mary and Christ Child scenes in churches and she, too, crafting beautifully colored glasswork in these woods of a remote corner of Vermont that Press wondered whether he might be scammed. Was she using her kids as a cover to case and rob his house? No valuables, no money to speak of hidden around because a teller he trusted at the bank ladled out the petty cash he needed when the Clarks drove him into town. As if sensing that his enthusiastic welcome was cooling, however, Carol remarked laughingly, "No, not on a first date. You can't come in the bathroom when I'm bathing," but started running the tub.

"We're Catholics," she said—her father and her, the whole big family, eight siblings.

He waited out her lengthy bath. "Delicious!" she yelled from the tub. "Thank you. I'm taking my time." The children had found the banty rooster,

23

hens, chicks, and eggs in the barn, and Karl's Percheron in the pasture, along with half a dozen heifers he was boarding for a friend; the bantys could fly and pretty much feed themselves all summer.

Carol microwaved the ground meat that was in its packet and explained that she had come north to the country from Dorothy Day's communitarian Catholic Worker movement on the Lower East Side in New York, where she'd helped in the soup kitchen, dormitory arrangements for homeless people, hospice visits, office cleaning, et cetera, with a guy from this commune, who was not the father of her children. No, Ten Mile Farm, as they called themselves, was not Catholic, she chuckled. "But we're doing our own thing."

He'd warmed to her again, hungry for a hug. And she divined this, and obliged, also explaining that she employed the techniques her father had taught her to fashion medallions, window hangings, and the like to sell at tourist stores or craft fairs, cutting her lovely supply of glass into shapes which were then soldered together with strips of lead.

"You can watch," she suggested, before catching herself and hugging him again.

"Am I an object of Christian charity?" he teased.

"Sure. By all means. And since I'm broke I am too. Like two peas in a pod. And I don't mind a lech as long as I can get away from him," she said, stepping aside from his groping hands. "Do sit down. I'll make burgers. I found frozen peas and corn. Supper's in half an hour."

The kids were now glued to the TV, another treat, yet amused and sorry at how close Press needed to kneel to look at the screen. This rigmarole had become an anguishing demonstration for his two at home. Carol vs. Claire: Too bad their names were so similar, but whoa, were they different! Claire, status-conscious, perfectionist, a statistician, Ivy-oriented, aiming for the top for her offspring. He enjoyed the school-talk and the meal, staying off communes or Catholicism, or anything else that might rock the boat. He was very happy, and when she'd washed the dishes and he'd dried them and she extracted her reluctant youngsters from the TV room, Press felt vaguely frantic to nail down another day when she'd return. Calmly, Carol wouldn't, though kissed him once she was back in the car.

"But how will I sculpt you?" he begged at the window.

She laughed. "In your mind's eye. Or else get clay, or use, maybe, rubber bands and a pillow." She took pity however and placed one of his hands on her breasts; then drove away.

Neighbors notice cars in your driveway, so Press had to parry the Swinnertons' curiosity. Did he have a cleaning woman? No? Did he *want* a cleaning woman? They recognized Carol's

25

car as local, not a visitor's from his previous life, remembered his questions about an unknown woman, but tactfully did not connect the dots, except for Karl's twitting Press about the possibility he would quit eating his lunches with them.

"No, no." Press looked forward to his wobbly bike rides—though the landscape had become impressionistic, eliding realistic detail—and being nuzzled by Sheila, their setter bitch, who unlike the hounds wasn't chained, and Dorothy's main flock of chickens clucking around the porch, a pet goat butting him deliberately, gently, and the two talkative pigs being raised for pork. Lolling in a sling chair, he'd let her draw him onto subjects like how New York had changed since she sold Christmas trees on the sidewalk at Twenty-Third Street, or what it felt like to first land in Paris on a vacation. Quebec City, not so far away, had sparked that dream. She wanted his problems solved, as did Karl, except the physical was so central to Karl that when you lost your "wind," as he called his growing emphysema worries, related possibly to firefighting, although he smoked as well, or for Press, your sight, hope was gone; you were a casualty. Because they cared, perhaps, they wondered for his own protection, about the advent of a hippie car in his drive. He didn't tipple at lunch in their house—did he drink or do something else at other hours? Karl had been through AA himself after the war, and knew about fraternizing with exotic locals. He was not a prude, but wasn't Press a sitting duck for somebody? Rich guy to gull.

*Gull me,* thought Press, when he heard the term. And Carol showed up briefly, as if bush telegraph had burned her ears. "Did I tease you too much? Did we eat up all your food?"

"No, no, I want to be teased."

She just brushed his cheek with a kiss. "I was a model in art school for years, so maybe I'm turning the tables. Naked man thinks of his girlfriend. I'll draw you some time if you're good." But unsexily she piled him in her Ford, drove him to market to replenish his groceries according to what he dictated should fill the cart, and ensured he got proper change for a fifty-dollar bill. Only back home did she revert to type for a moment. "Mew like a kitten," she said while restocking his fridge and shelves. He wanted her to cook, so she did, but as further reward brushed his hand across her breasts again. "I'm your siren. Think about it."

The public sighting reached the Clarks' ears, who worried less for his purse than his soul. They hoped the car was a cleaning woman's—he needed one—even if she were a hippie as Avis Clark put it, though like the Swinnertons, they didn't personally know the Ten Mile Farm hippies, except for selling them milk or picking up

27

a hitchhiker. Preferring not to think ill of new neighbors, they had reported at the church that the young folks up the hill were trying to find themselves, and "counterculture" was a sensible word, all things considered. Who, if they thought about it, at the Solid Rock in sincere attendance, wasn't also? Yet Avis had placed Press on her personal prayer list of eight people she mentioned to God at several junctures every day. She wanted him cared for as darkness descended upon his life. Housework, cooking, cleaning—it should be a local person known for a hard-work ethic and honest with money, but who was this youngish lady nobody knew ferrying him shopping, which they'd usually done?

Darryl felt the same, although his idea of who to suggest was different. At church, nobody had volunteered for a daily commitment, partly because husbands didn't want their women working for a single man, so Darryl suggested an old crone named Melba, penniless in old age but an "adventuress," as Avis deemed her. She'd been in the West, but had returned to wind up in a trailer on the property of Rupert, an auctioneer and cattle dealer whose mistress she had once been, maybe as far back as school. For all Avis knew, Darryl might have lost his cherry to her too. Rupert had a wife and was retired, having given the auction barn and commission sales enterprise to his son Rog, but at the far end of his land he let Melba inhabit a dented house trailer hired hands had made the best of through many years. He gave her lifts to town to fill her larder, mad as his wife was about it.

"She can scrub," Darryl said. "And it's so close she can use that unregistered car she's got. No tags but nobody'll see it."

True. And she'd lost her looks long ago. Rupert himself probably didn't fancy her now either, though when she'd left Athol she'd been his agent out West, shipping him carloads of Herefords or broncs to sell here. But she'd long since fallen on hard times and Avis was against siccing her at poor Press. Darryl was set on Melba earning some pocket cash, so long as they could kind of ride herd on her, so they compromised by tipping Melba off to Press's situation without accompanying her as guarantors when she tried to sell herself.

Thus Press, who had been impatiently twiddling his thumbs, waiting for Carol's raspy, aged Ford Maverick—or was it a Pinto?—to return after the last time, heard instead another wheezy motor pull in. He might have worried it was swampers, people-smugglers, except the sun was still high. The car door slammed weakly and her footsteps were light. "I can scrub good," her voice announced, plausibly more than twice Carol's age. "Your neighbors said you could stand a bit of help?"

He invited Melba onto the porch, and when told he was a city boy, she said, "Yeah, well I've been in cities. LA, Vegas, you name it." When he was silent, she added, "I know you can't see. I won't hold that against you, but I always look at a man's teeth. I've bought so many teeth."

"Really?"

"Yeah. Cowboys. They break their teeth and if you're with them you got to buy 'em new ones. Making motel beds to buy them teeth. I'm speaking of the circuit. Not wranglers as much as rodeo cowboys. A bull rider will break his front teeth and you don't want to look at it all the time."

"I believe you," Press said. "I bet."

"Five dollars an hour." He heard her walk inside, open cupboards and drawers, tromp upstairs, then fill the sink. "Should I plunge ahead? We're both straight shooters." Didn't even wait for his answer.

"So, how many cowboys?" he asked, joining her in the kitchen.

"Bulldoggers. Bronc-busters. It wasn't just cowboys. Oh, I'd sleep in the straw at Santa Anita. Horsemen; Rupert was like that. Cows were his meat and potatoes—selling them. But he liked horses. I'd send him a carload right off the range. Still has a couple running wild in his woods that nobody would buy. They come to my door when they're lonesome for a touch, even if I don't have oats."

"Do you have enough for yourself?" Press asked, hearing poverty in her voice.

"Oh, baby, I sleep on cans. That's my bedstead, cartons o' cans. The bedsprings, the mattress is on top of that. I'm not fat, but you'll never catch me without any food. I used to be able to hitchhike at the drop of a hat. Anywhere at all. The first trucker would stop. But I wouldn't get in if he didn't look like he'd buy me a burger down the road." She laughed. "He might have, too."

"I'm a believer," Press agreed, the same line he employed at the Solid Rock Church, though she had never heard him say it there. She bustled with broom, sponge, and mop, remembering other men in trouble she'd helped. "One poor sap had got butt-fucked so much in prison his sad ass looked like a cunt. So sore his poor little pecker wouldn't stand up any more. But I cured him," she muttered.

Gingerly, Press brought up the subject of children by way of asking if she had any grandchildren.

"Sons grow up trying to be like their daddy—which you didn't think of when you'd possibly picked the man. But grandsons may break the mold and go to college, or whatever." One of hers had, as far as she'd heard. "We lived in the sticks, though, when I had babies. You're trying to help the father, not realizing it ain't good for the son."

Benny "The Bear" Messer had been a favorite of hers here, growing up, like Rupert, while Karl

Swinnerton was playing soldier boy and Darryl Clark was a Future Farmer of America. Benny raced cars and piled up junk, playing mechanic without wanting to open a garage. "He'd chop up stolen cars. I told him that in LA such cars were *worth* chopping up, but he was a stick-in-the-mud like Darryl—stayed right where he was born. And when he played chicken with the other boys, he never chickened out—stayed right on that center line, like a bat outa hell. Cops couldn't outrun him either, just wait for him at home."

"And he was stubborn too when he got down in my spring-hole to dig the rocks out."

"That's Benny, yes, he's a bear. And he's got any old part your car needs. That's where his mind is. Always looking out the window at his cars.

"Never had a wife. Oh, he'd screw you with the best of them and still could hang a towel on his cock, but then his mind wanders out to that junkyard. Like Karl, with his trapline and hound dogs, bird dogs, Benny would take some patience, without being a solid citizen like Karl is. War hero, and the fire stuff—he saved the church steeple. Me, I've fucked up my life good, and nothing to show for it."

She finished what she felt up to doing today, and Press, with an inkling that Carol might come today, was eager for them not to meet.

"Want me back?" she questioned.

"Yes," he assented, and gave Melba what he

hoped, and she said, was the right-sized bill, whereupon her gears ground noisily away. Benny would make her fuck her eyes out to fix it, she had claimed. And Wanda, Rupert's long-suffering wife, hated having her live on his property, the Clarks said. Press wondered how old she was, or looked, as he waited for his hunch about Carol's approach to prove out, but she didn't come.

# Chapter 2

Not the Clarks but Dorothy and Karl took him to the evening auction sales. At 8 p.m., with no movie house in town, people congregated Tuesday on the short set of bleachers facing a wooden ring in which aging dairy cows were sold, mainly for hamburger, and vealer calves, also for slaughter, if not singled out by a farmer rebuilding his herd. Rival buyers from meat companies in Massachusetts bid against each other for the frightened cows, mooing instead of lowing—old matrons who might have been leading a barn full of milkers out to pasture every day and back but had outlived their peak productivity and now were being disposed of. Crammed into an unfamiliar pen with strangers of their ilk, dominant till this morning but milling, terrified, they were in pain as well from not having been milked.

Press couldn't see this, but heard all of it once Dorothy interpreted. The calves bleating, a few weeks old, and Rog, Rupert's son the auctioneer, peremptory as a sergeant keeping order. Both Swinnertons had an expert eye for what an individual cow would weigh and her age and condition, but also how the farm family sitting there near them might feel watching her go to be ground up to be served on a bun with fries if they'd owned her. "It's like taking your old car to the crusher," said Karl.

"Good blood sausage there," Rog barked harshly. "Don't throw out the innards." Rog was a better businessman than Rupert, Dorothy said, but people liked him less. Then, in fact, Rupert introduced himself to Press via a rough hand, at Melba's urging. When Press asked if she was with him, "No. Wanda," Rupert specified ironically.

A wheelbarrow was auctioned, a box of quacking ducks, some lawn furniture, and a bag of squawking chickens, in Dorothy's description. Kids clambered up and down the shaky bleacher boards, while the little crowd bantered with Rog's interpretation of his miscellany. A case of motor oil, truck tires, three Seiko watches ("Not hot, but warm"), and other stuff: to vary the procession of woeful, doleful, panicked cows being prodded offstage into livestock eighteen-wheelers for the trip to the slaughterhouse.

"Look at the boobs on that lady, though!" Rog might interrupt his conventional spiel when a particularly udderly cow bolted into the ring. "You don't want her throat cut yet, do you? Buy her for the farm. She'll keep the milk truck coming. She's got Holstein written all over her. The guy that owns her's going out of business and he needs the money for the poker game."

Like Rupert before him, Rog held a wee-hours game in his office after the show, at which sellers could lose what they'd earned earlier in the night. He was ruder, more grasping than Rupert, Karl said, but his patter was better and the bookkeepers were his mom, Wanda, and his Quebecoise wife, Juliette, who was invaluable when dealing with French-language folk, who may have farmed here for forty years without learning English. And when you died, whether Yankee or French, Rog and his wife would show up to persuade your widow into selling cheap everything they could, in her grief and a necessity for cash, before the children arrived from California, or wherever they'd moved, to lend her some guidance. Land, house, and cattle.

"He's a vulture," Karl said. "But also a good fireman. Maybe he thinks there'll be jewels in the ashes." But he added, "No, he's okay, a pretty good man. He's backed me up." Meaning in the famous steeple fire Karl and his cohorts were known for, when they saved the church, people in the village said.

Rog sold a bull; then a pony. When Rupert's voice interrupted, kibitzing occasionally, Rog shook him off. "Look at that little brown Jersey. Wouldn't she fit in your boudoir nicely?" Rupert couldn't top lines like that. They were both ladies' men, roaming the roads to pick out bargains, but that French wife kept a tighter rein on Rog.

"Hey, there's hippies here," Karl mentioned. "I guess they come to buy goats to milk, bedsteads, and tomato plants. Maybe your girlfriend'll come over."

But she didn't.

"Sorry," she said, showing up unexpectedly early the next morning when Press was carefully heating water for coffee. "I haven't been away but I've been dealing with the guy that built my house. He seems to think I owe him forever." She actually hugged Press, didn't merely tease him with a grope. They sat. She asked for news of his own two kids, Jeremy and Molly. Hers were at a friend's house.

Suddenly, as the silence grew vaguely embarrassing, she said, "I'll take you home." He didn't understand what that meant till he found himself winding up a short braiding of dirt roads to the small cabin he'd been near when he climbed along the stream, then settled in a threadbare upholstered chair of the sort you might salvage from the front lawn of a foreclosed house.

"This is what I do all day," she said—meaning cut and manipulate stained glass. And he began to hear the click of tools, smelled the soldering iron.

"Not so bad?" she asked after a spell.

"No, no, I could spend an eternity in this chair, I guess, unless your patience wore out."

She repaid the compliment by regretting he couldn't see her work. "But this is what I do. And I'm sick of being hit on. I suppose that's partly why I like you, because you can't." She laughed,

37

moving over to poke her finger in his mouth to suck on like a cigarette. "And yet I hit on you myself."

She rolled a joint, from the crinkle that he heard, and then the scent. "I need to wean this other guy off me."

He smiled. "I hope so." Carol continued working, after offering Press a cookie and tea. Eventually her concentration waned and she sat down with a sigh and said, "I have something for you." He listened, hesitating stupidly for more of a hint while she waited.

"Are you not interested?"

He walked toward her voice, then, her shape apparitional in the other chair.

"I need a body rub," she instructed. "I want to be spoiled." He obliged, luxuriating. Afterward, she fed him peanut butter and jelly on hamburger rolls, which they ate by the stream, and drove him home before the kids returned.

For the whole next day he remained jubilant, alone, apologizing to the Swinnertons by phone for missing two lunches with them, but Dorothy said Karl was butchering a deer he'd shot and they were busy anyway with preserving the cuts of that, from lard and heart to chitterlings. He listened to Mozart and Bach broadcast from Montreal, combined with the creak of his swing on the porch, barn swallows harvesting bugs overhead, a teacher bird, and a wood thrush's liquid fluting.

Jack Brook rushed tumbling down the mildish mountainside that led to Carol's cabin. He wondered if he simply climbed it again and yelled for her, she'd hear him. If he turned an ankle, of course, no one might find him for several days, because she wouldn't be notified that he was missing by Karl or whoever was faced by the quandary. Karl had often searched for missing persons in his heyday, with Fish and Game, the sheriff, or the state cops, using a hound he'd trained. Another hound would trail whichever furbearer he was after at that moment in the snow—leaving a raccoon's track, for instance, if he pointed at a fox's prints they crossed, which was more valuable, but then leaving the fox's, perhaps, if Karl saw a bobcat's, whose skin would fetch still more cash: as much as sixty dollars. A miracle dog, she could also smell and tell him which mink or beaver traps had a creature in them. Tree frogs and leopard frogs were singing, along with the birds, and Press was grateful to Karl for teaching him the distinctions—also peepers, toads, green frogs. Dorothy had written a column on the subject from Karl's explanation; then later one on missing-person searches, when Press had drawn him conversationally out on *that*. What lost people did in circling, or where a murder victim had been dumped. In the war, Karl been a BAR man, toting that extra-heavy Browning automatic, bi-pod rifle; another story altogether. He didn't discuss combat or recount how he had won his Bronze Star, nor want her to write about it. Just fire prevention, drawing on his recent expertise.

"You're a breath of fresh air," Dorothy told Press, meaning his knack for suggesting ideas for pieces for the local paper she had overlooked— like the novel viewpoint those summer boarders from the city had brought to her parents' farm when she was young.

Press felt energized by Carol's opening to him, and Dorothy's approval, Karl's savvy and sympathetic stoicism, and the Clarks' dependable support. Those multiple hugs in the Solid Rock Gospel pews solaced him too. And you didn't know, or need to know, whether the lady was "pretty," but maybe recognized her perfume from last week. Twice a week he went with Avis and Darryl to church, often sharing a potluck supper there after the service, or doing his shopping and mailing a check Avis had helped him fill out and sign. No call for Meals on Wheels or social worker visits, at least so far. The principal drag on his spirits remained only the inevitable pain of losing his children for this extended period. How could they visit him under the circumstances, and his daily phone calls at homework time were turning dutiful at their end, when they reported their assignments and so on, which he seldom could help with. Their friendships he remembered were also turning passé. His night dreams when peopled with them tended to be affectionately reassuring, however. The one thorn in his shoe at night, so to speak, were occasional outside sounds. The tattoo of owl hoots from down in the swamp were fine, but the rasp of an ATV vehicle or faint shout after dark was not. Did he even hear footfalls on the trail his driveway led to, and then a car engine start on the road, as though a passenger had been picked up?

To live in a bootlegger's old house had its ghosts, indoors and out, but what did it mean in terms of action now? And who could he ask? Karl as a fire chief cooperated with lawmen on suicides, lost hunters, suspicious fires, and ambulance calls, yet he also shot deer out of season and resented the Customs and Immigration vans that serviced the barrier and motion sensors blocking entry to Canada at the border on Ten Mile Road. It had never had a booth there, but people formerly could cross. The dead "Chinaman" hadn't roused him to call the authorities, while the Clarks, for their part, seemed to have woven a Christian cocoon around their farm, regardless of outlaw neighbors like Karl's dad and grandpa or lately the hippies. See and hear no evil was their solution to ambiguity when no neat wraparound answer, like asking Melba to clean for Press, was at hand. If Press continued to rub shoulders at the commune, it was his lookout, not theirs.

He did find an opportunity to tell them he'd never set foot at the commune, though hoping in the meantime that Carol would soon lead him there to further their intimacy. Her cabin by choice was the furthest outlier, almost out of earshot of the wilder pot-and-acid parties. Being a mother, she didn't indulge in the latter. Sin you rebuff but not the sinners, so he hadn't fallen from the Clarks' good graces, not being a drunk or pothead himself. Yet monkey business in the swamp seemed a gripe not right to tattle about to them. Was it worse than the senior Swinnertons brewing corn whiskey and bathtub beer next door, or Benny Messer slicing up stolen cars with his torch, or Rog or Rupert soliciting a blow job from a widow foreclosed on by the bank, without two pennies to rub together, only some torpid cows and spastic furniture to auction?

So, no fantasies verging on paranoia about night sounds from the swamp. It could be a raven quarreling with a loon, a porcupine with a skunk, not Mafia dons. Carol, wholesome like a mom, turned up with her youngsters for an ice cream and pizza outing. Then they discovered a trunk in the attic with dress-up clothes. The ladder itself was a scary delight, and the shade trees around his house were a different challenge to climb from the forest softwoods surrounding their cabin. "Not as cozy," Carol claimed, but they didn't agree. She herself, in a hot bath—letting him "watch"—later admitted his place was comfier, "But you're not trying to change the world."

Press couldn't see if she was smiling in hippie presumptuousness or speaking straight-faced. "No, I'm in survival mode," he said.

"Well, I'm here to testify you're going to survive. And you can scrub my back if you want. Only that. I still want to draw you, when I have a chance. *Naked Man Thinks of His Girlfriend.* Then we'll sell it at a garage sale."

Hearing the kids, he wished his own Jeremy could know her boy, Tim, and Molly know Christie. Maybe in a perfect world it would happen, family on a visit. But now she took them home.

Next day, he biked to the Swinnertons for shepherd's pie. Often eating took considerably extra time, since he could hardly see his food, groping with a fork or spoon, enforceably omnivorous. "Blind men wear spotted pants," Dorothy teased, telling him to wash his—and what he called "Sheila time," petting the dog, who reminded him of the English setter he loved as a boy. Afterward, Melba was his only visitor. She wanted "macaroni money. But I don't take charity. And although I'll grant you I handled plenty of boners in my time, I never turned a trick."

"Good," Press responded, and explained when she asked that his name was short for Prescott.

"Never heard that one. Sounds like a senator's

moniker. Although I do admit that when some red-haired trucker gives you a lift from Elko to Council Bluffs, what are you gonna offer him? If that counts." She began to work like a beetle. "Depends what counts," she added. "These rich ladies that marry money—what are they doing? Or this hippie I hear is hauling your ashes?"

"I wish." He laughed. He liked Melba, and pumped her for more information about Rupert and Rog than the Swinnertons or Clarks had provided. Did they prey on widows, for instance?

"Well, we're all widows nowadays," she answered sarcastically. "No, Rupert was a nicer guy than Rog. He liked horses, he liked old things. Had a whetstone of mine back in the woods. His idea of a square deal might not have been yours, but it wasn't a scam. And you'd like his younger son, Al. He hauls the cows down to Springfield to the knackers. Gives them their last ride. But up in front he'll have a hippie with him sometimes that wants a lift closer to the cities. From Springfield they can catch a bus to Albany or Bridgeport or Boston or wherever their folks live. He's not prejudiced against strangers like the rest of these Woodchucks, or some. I'm a Woodchuck too. And he'll tuck some pot in with the cow shit for them, because the cops don't inspect a cow truck."

But when he pushed for more, "Ask your girlfriend where they grow it," she told him. "Rog is not the worst in the world either. He'll spring for a loan, although like anybody, depends on who you are."

Press recited a few dicey aspects of the fix *he* was in, and his father's death from bowel cancer last year, to persuade her of a sympathetic ear should she open up her litany of woes the Clarks had hinted at. She just murmured "Funerals," however, as if that covered it.

Hated to see a front-end loader. A son of hers had been riding for fun in the bucket of a tractor his father was driving and flipped out when it hit a bump. Her footsteps—the very shape of her body in relief against a window—changed as she recounted it. He didn't mention that he'd heard wild gossip that she'd had a baby killed by a pig, but did tell Melba that he had skied at Aspen and visited Yellowstone, so knew the big skies she must love.

"Yeah, no, these people don't know shit," she said. "Some of them have never seen the Atlantic Ocean in Maine or a mountain worth the name."

"It's lonely, huh?" Press agreed, though maybe less so when all was said and done. Sleeping on a bed of canned foodstuffs beneath the springs, with three unsold Wyoming broncs nosing at the window for company. Hard-bitten, indeed.

"Critters help." She liked orange cats. But when he used that opening to bring up the sounds from the swamp, she interjected, "Critters are pretty vocal if you're not accustomed to them. They go north and south. We even get seagulls that fly all the way in to scrounge at the river or the dump."

"But I mean, not animal."

"Well." She hesitated. "You're an innocent bystander. You're not responsible for what you don't know."

"Should I call the cops?"

She chuckled. "You'd lose that status, wouldn't you then, in every direction?" She had no phone, she added, when he asked about calling her. And Rupert was not a law and order man either. "But who's going to bother a blind guy, anyhow? He'd sell you a pistol!" She reminded him that since Karl knew the swamp best, "Why not ask him? Isn't life mostly grinning and bearing it?"

Press produced a bottle of vodka—"against my better judgment"—and tonic water to share with her before she left; it did break some ice. "You're not in AA, are you?"

"Hardly." Though Melba didn't unburden herself of family memories, she spoke about how measly it had felt to work making beds in a gambling town like Reno or Las Vegas where high rollers, mobsters, and businessmen were throwing money away like confetti, while the cowboy she was partnered with busting his butt for a third-place purse.

He bemoaned missing the childhoods of Jeremy and Molly, but Melba said, "They'll love you when they know you."

"This is your big day. You're in luck," Carol announced, showing up with Tim and Christie in the car on Saturday. He climbed in when invited to.

"We're going to The Farm," she finally disclosed as they arrived. Other kids greeted hers, and led Press, curiously, carefully, to a homemade-feeling rocking chair on a porch.

"Everybody wanted to see what a stockbroker looked like. I'll bring you some tea. And let me know if you need to pee. I'll be with friends." She disappeared.

So there he sat. People coming and going said hello. It seemed a central domicile, of two stories, by the clump on the stairs inside and clink of kitchenware. Children whose voices he didn't recognize brought him some flowers to smell, telling each other he was blind—then snapped at a kid who apparently was planning to test him with a bit of chicken shit.

A tyke climbed into his lap. Carol had told him earlier that hard-core commune ideologues believed all of the children here belonged equally to all of the adults. One extremist even thought the same about getting pregnant she said; or maybe simply wanted to ensure that no man would ever come knocking on her door someday demanding visitation rights. She organized a sort of circle-jerk at her house, where five reasonably agreeable guys jacked off, whether one by one or all together, into a salad bowl, and she stirred the resulting stew of jism with a turkey baster to fertilize herself. "You should have been there. You could have made a little Prescott, and no child support. Just a community mom."

People stopped to tell him they knew his place, or had passed him on his bike, and were glad he was visiting. Was he staying for the sweat lodge? "Saturday nights is Sweat Lodge."

"Sure," Carol informed him when he asked, bringing him a glass of tea and chunk of jack cheese in a hamburger bun. Also she took him to a patch of brush behind the farmhouse to piss, holding him by the arm as he did so.

"Show it to me," she said. "I'm going to see it anyhow tonight."

He heard another person moving beside them, afterward, and when he'd sat down again, a woman pulled a chair over and chatted with him for a while. From Chicago, a leather maker, she checked his politics, educational level, age, immediate history, and social status and asked about how he had gone blind. Saying she was going to sew a belt for him, she had him stand and pinched and plumbed his waist and elsewhere.

"Handsome" was her verdict to Carol. "Cheers for you. And I kind of like that he's blind, if not hereditary."

Men talked to him as well, confirming perhaps

48

that he truly couldn't see and wasn't just a narc in disguise. A black-bearded fellow he understood to be the leader, "The Dad," squatted and gripped Press's knee strongly while quizzing him about being a "moneyman," before chuckling and deciding he could stay, at least for today. Besides the commune's leatherwork, there was a potter who had a kiln, and two men who logged with local outfits in the woods. Other members commuted to earn wages nursing, waitressing, carpentering, or whatever.

Carol returned and led him toward the former dairy barn, now compartmentalized into a dozen living quarters, high and low. Her children were playing outside, when not running back to the house or up a dirt track to somebody else's log hut, tent, wigwam, or dome, as she described it. He could see the outline of a tepee, himself.

"Let's go see your friend," Carol said. "By the way, it occurred to me, aren't you afraid your kids may inherit eye problems like you?"

"No, no. It's called serpiginous choroiditis and is episodic; it scars your retinas. It's not from your genes."

Within the murmurous old barn—homey conversations left and right from the relic hayloft up above—she steered him to a wooden ladder. "Now climb. I'm right behind you. You're safe."

He didn't feel safe, although she patted his ass and though the woman who had questioned him on the porch said from the top, "Right as rain. All ready for you." As she was, gripping his hands as he drew close, while Carol gently teased his balls from below to keep him progressing without pause. "Good boy."

It was a flat floor with no rail he could distinguish, so he stayed on all fours, groping forward, and they let him, their legs directing him, upright on both sides, till he met a pile of quilts and comforters and pillows, and stopped. "Yes," Carol assured him. "Wasn't so bad. You made it. Be comfortable. The scary part's over."

The two women, flanking him, sat cross-legged, and talked in normal tones about commune news, who was heading for New York or arguing with the Athol school board. Maybe half an hour of gossip went by before he felt his pants unbuttoned and skinned off. "Is he wired for a nipple?" the other woman said. Carol laughed. "You'll see."

He could hear their smiles form as his wiring proved apt. A hard cock, and he smelled Vaseline, and somebody rubbed it with that.

"Isn't it funny how forty years after they suckled, it's still so central to them. I should rent him out. This lady wants a baby without the hassle," Carol explained to Press. "The state pays for it, and there's no lug around. We'll babysit. An Ivy League father, no less." But such practical talk didn't short-circuit his mounting her ample friend and beginning to pump.

"Sweet boy." Carol was touched. "You don't have to satisfy her. Don't worry, it's the delivery that counts." He felt his back stroked and his buttocks gripped in silence by the lady under him. It was fast, like a stolen quickie in a closet, but as intense as bright light shearing off sheet metal; when Carol recognized he was about to come, "Give it to her! Give it to her!" she urged, like a jockey. "Deep in, deep in. Stay with her. Let 'em swim! Please stay in," she repeated when he felt ready to withdraw.

The lady, still nameless, stayed put when Press sat up. Carol produced a Hershey bar for him, and brewed hot chocolate on a hissing Coleman stove while he caught his breath. She joked with her friend about a lesbian commune, over a few of Vermont's hills from them, which had imported a presentable young man somebody knew to do the same for all of them, then "let him go," so that they could all experience pregnancy, childbirth, and motherhood together.

She touched Press affectionately and handed him his pants. They lingered, resting from their secret adventure, in the dimly filtered sunlight, listening to the nesting swallows, nesting rodents. He was sworn to confidentiality.

Eventually they went to supper at the farm-house, separately, so that Press wouldn't pick up further clues about his paramour's identity. Rice and salad, and everybody holding hands in a circle before and after eating. The bread of course fresh from the oven, and a flock of chickens had provided an egg custard enriched with maple syrup. The meat-eaters had some venison they'd fried, but Press pretended to vegetarianism, like the majority. On the porch outside, again he rode with the flow in his rocking chair, except for turning down the tokes that were proffered, but not asking to be driven home.

Bonfires had been lit. It was Sweat Lodge Night, the kids were perfectly in their element, running from family huddle to family huddle in the sunset, welcome everywhere, penned in nowhere, and a donkey brayed, between giving them rides. He heard a softball game going on, but Carol led him to the creek near where the sweathouse was to laze because she liked the swirl of running water, though this was not her own. "If you're scared, you can go," she promised again, "otherwise, it's so warm we could be here till dawn." Her kids were on a sleepover.

"No, I'm with you," he pledged, "yummy." She napped, arms outflung, the temperature was so inviting, then supervised three dog-paddlers in the stream. Men were heating the stones to dump into the chute that created the sweathouse steam, so she crawled inside after stripping, with Press holding onto her ankles, through the claustro-phobic igloo-style entrance hole. But he panicked inside. Would it grow unbearably hot, or the plywood structure even catch fire? And since he couldn't see, how could he escape? But she'd sensed his fear and directed him out, whereupon he couldn't find his clothes. A stranger had to give them to him, sans wallet, which turned out to have fallen on the ground.

When Carol emerged at last, as wet as a seal with sweat, she cradled him—"Old man left his comfort zone!"—and pulled him into the creek with her.

"So," she asked, "Home? Soaked. Scared?"

"I'd be so lonely," he said. "But yes."

"Doesn't want to go home, but's scared of these wild hippies. Okay, I'll draw you, like I thought. I was in art school, you know."

She took him to her cabin, lit the kerosene lamp and candles. "Okeydokey, clothes off again, sir. Like a lost little sheep. You're not on Wall Street anymore. You're in the hands of a bossy artist."

Possibly a couple of hours passed in being sketched. He couldn't view the results, however, but fell asleep on her couch until she delivered him to his house en route to retrieving her family from their sleepover. The morning light was lovely, and the solidity of a real, hundred-year-old, single-family home seemed priceless, before he sensed—realized—recognized that somebody had been inside during the night. The refrigerator had been raided and food left about, the telephone disturbed in its location, and he fingered the imprint of a burly body marked in the leather chair. Yet not a robbery. The drawers weren't pulled out; no creepy feeling upstairs, just downstairs, as if somebody had hiked up from the swamp, made a call, fortified himself with sandwich meat, and moved along.

Gracious, if only Carol had shared his discovery, helped him search the house and outbuildings— suppose it became sort of a depot? He might have called his neighbors promptly, except he would have needed to explain he'd been away spending all night with the hippies. Calling 911, though, would put the incident on the radio scanner and also into Karl and Dorothy's living room. "Think a while," he told himself. No malice, no personal acquaintance was indicated; nothing broken, no harm done. It could have been a stranger passing through, assuming this was just a summer person's empty hideaway. On the other hand, some Ten Mile Farm commune druggie, noticing him there, might have arranged a pickup from Canada while Carol had him in tow. Actually, Melba was the one he wanted advice from, but, like Carol, she had no phone. Would she suggest he buy that pistol from Rupert, or rent the upstairs for protection? A blind man shooting at sounds would be bad news.

He calmed down, biked as usual to the Swinnertons' for lunch, but although loose lips sink ships, over the rhubarb sauce, he couldn't keep his buttoned. Karl's reaction to what he blurted was "People now!" Dorothy sounded less surprised, and took up his idea of a housemate; "You could advertise." Neither rudely asked where Press had been, but it occurred to him that a renter upstairs would cramp his style when Carol dropped in. Having a live-in housekeeper for companionship had crossed his mind as an option his income might warrant. He'd postponed the thought.

"I'd like to lie there with a rifle," Karl said. "If anybody plans on coming back. But I think I'd ride with it for now."

He sat with them for a long time, collecting aplomb, not least because Karl began spinning tales of the Abenaki Indians here. Their arrowheads and pestles could be found at campsites left behind. And Rogers's Rangers raiding Canada in the French and Indian War had dashed down through the swamp. Also high-quality Scotch being smuggled to the fanciest clubs in New York City or Washington, DC, during Prohibition in the 1920s, then draft dodgers escaping conscription to Vietnam via the ten-mile trek to Canada quite recently. And barracks remained from when timber jacks extracted cedar oil or telephone poles, hemlock logs or white-pine flooring.

"Birch, spruce, fir," he said, as if demystifying the place for Press.

They strolled outdoors to change the subject,

visiting Karl's Percheron in the pasture, with endearments and some oats, plus the heifers he was raising for a friend. Dorothy's cat had followed them, hunting mice in the sun.

"Yep. I'm staying," Press decided, especially after calling Merrill Lynch ex-colleagues. Not that he could have returned to lunching at the Oyster Bar in Grand Central Station and hustling thousand-share lots to customers without being able to read the research materials—but the stress vibrating in these conversations reminded him of a job for which he'd been a square peg in a round hole, though slated to stay forever. This adventure wasn't preferable, but he wasn't so nostalgic for the job, just Jeremy and Molly and their family life.

When Press asked Darryl whether he had ever been robbed, "Everybody keeps a gun," he said. The Clarks would have called the sheriff, so he bit his tongue about the home invasion, holding them in abeyance as a resource, during the next church and market excursion they treated him to.

"I bet I could live in your barn, it's so peaceful. The smell of the hay, the cows munching or chewing their cuds a little, stirring around so comfortably, mooing to each other. Even the milking machines lull you if you're sitting."

"If you're not workin'," Avis answered. "But sit there till you're cured."

"We got a mongoose working for us. Pops in

and out of the bales. Kills more than the cats do, and they can't catch him," Darryl put in.

He meant a weasel, Avis explained. But at the church, Press wondered irrationally for a moment if he was being observed, and by whom, and as at the commune, then who he was holding hands with when the service was over.

To Melba, however, Press blabbed everything out, his worries and speculations, hoping her upside down worldliness might jigsaw into alignment with his. She disliked the hippies and sheriffs in equal measure, but did not demonize them. "The mobsters in Vegas, they don't kill the little people," she said. "Or those rotgut smugglers that were here, when they were kings, driving like mad. If you're just a disabled guy that draws walk-around money every week from the teller at the bank, who wants to hurt you? You don't keep your money in a sock, like the rest of us do."

"I'm not sure they're that logical."

"No. I guess not. Someone oughta live with you, but I don't want to." He hadn't asked, but nor would Carol probably. Tough it out? Man up!

"I wouldn't fret, but I'd call the cops," she advised. "That way, if they're in on it themselves, they'll know you're wise." The state police rotated in and out, so they were likely to be clean. "And they don't mess with little stuff either. But the sheriff before this one—he had an arrangement where he didn't notice a certain field where a

Piper Cub from Canada could land once in a while, under a mountain, below the radar. He didn't run again, but he didn't suffer for that either; moved to Florida. Maybe you just had a hungry hiker."

"So I shouldn't call the new one?"

"I'll get Rupert to. We'll widen the net. You'll never know who knew. But a blind man!" she added to comfort him. "Who'd beat up on him? Just keep your money in the bank." Men were like hound dogs at a strip show, she said, eyes begging, tongues hanging out, yet when money moved into the picture they turned mean. "So mean."

She laughed, recounting the meanness she had seen while cleaning a thousand people's motel rooms across the West. Blood from bloody noses, abandoned girlfriends, even children. Comatose patrons in their skivvies awaiting eviction, with coins and condoms on the floor. Veterans hallucinating, women hemorrhaging from abortions gone wrong, rich bastards dangling a hundred-dollar bill in front of her nose that they might leave as a tip if she put her tongue on their crotch. "No, flat out, I don't move in with guys anymore."

Not that Press had asked her, of course, but he *was* toying with the notion of inviting Carol's family to share his roomy home her kids had already enjoyed exploring so much. A sexy, far-fetched idea, to be sure, but also a selfish one if it would endanger them. And *should* his house thereby become a sort of branch of the commune?

Was he up for that? Forbidding visitations would be out of bounds.

"Not that I like to talk to Rupert, especially, but I'll tell him. Macaroni money," she called the bill he gave her. "Most of us live on the edge."

That night, he heard both great horned owls hooting from the swamp and barred owls from the mountainside, grateful for Karl's instruction and the bird-call tape a friend had sent him. A porcupine was methodically chewing on the salty, oily floorboards of his garage, then quarreling in high-pitched, abbreviated whines with another. Salts were needed for digesting bark, their main diet, Karl had said, and Press heard them rattling their quills aggressively at each other. This somehow prompted the idea of a ruse  buying an old heap from Benny Messer to park in his drive so it looked occupied, as if people were at home.

"Hey," Benny responded when Press called from the Swinnertons'. "It's on me. I'll loan you a loaner! In fact, I'll rig up a shotgun on that trail that'll blow anybody's head off that trips the wire. I've got a goose gun perfect for that!"

"No, please, the car, not the gun," Press insisted, as the Swinnertons listened, chuckling, over lunch. Karl took out a goose gun, long-barreled, to show him, three shells in the magazine, so you could subtract three from a low-flying chevron.

# Chapter 3

Lounging at home the next morning, he was surprised to hear Carol's car, and then her footsteps, so female. His juices, his longing, flowed, and when she hugged him, his hands tried to slide down her backside, but she shook him off. "I'm depressed." She led him to the couch, sat beside him, and leaned her head on his shoulder, but then laid it in his lap. "My father would do this," she mentioned.

"And . . . what?" Press gently suggested.

"My mistakes! Wasting time. Who's going to buy glass in the sticks like this?"

He couldn't argue to the contrary, imagining how paltry the few crafts fairs must be hereabouts. He scratched her scalp, stroked her neck.

"Also the *kids!* No father." Unlike some of the other ladies, Carol wanted to know who their father was, and for them to eventually—she had picked the gentleman, a poet in New York, also an alumnus of Dorothy Day's Catholic Worker movement, who hadn't wanted to try the country, though, like her. And she'd returned to him again for Christie to be fertilized, even knowing he was going to stay on the Lower East Side, doing both work for Dorothy and dealing in pot on the side. Now her children had no man at Ten Mile Farm who, when he looked at them, registered them as his. "That may be convenient for me sometimes, but it's bad for them."

Press didn't demur. The father was a good poet, apparently, and better, she thought, than any artist here, but your genetics were incomplete; a child should have someone to run to for hugs.

He forbore murmuring "How about me?" Just rubbed her scalp, fingered her hair, and told her to listen to the indigo bunting. Besides pleased that she had turned to him when blue, he was relieved because her trust erased the gnawing suspicion he had harbored that she could be in league with a commune plot to sneak drugs through his property. Indeed, the sheriff and Rupert arrived while they were innocently communing, the sheriff younger and raspier-voiced than old rascally Rupert. By their questions, both seemed primarily interested in sizing up Press, rather than the home invasion, and now in his relationship to this younger woman. Was she a live-in, a hippie, or a relative? Press recited for the sheriff a resume of his life preceding Vermont, and Rupert offered to take him to the dump to shoot rats if he wanted, then was embarrassed because Melba had already told him Press was blind.

"She said you have a seeing-eye dog," he said rudely, meaning Carol, to cover his blunder; however, then made up for it by asking if Press would like to go anyway, since "In my dotage I'm Waste Commissioner."

"Nearly finished him." The sheriff laughed. "The Cat plumb threw him off. And he lay under the fucking blade with the engine roaring for a couple of hours before anybody discovered him, with the tracks trying to get a purchase the whole time."

Rupert humphed as though glad and sheepish in equal measure to hear his ordeal recounted. "Well, it's a big change for you," he said to shift the topic to Press. "Melba says you *do* know your ass from a hole in the ground."

"I hope so."

"Swamps are kind of a law unto themselves," the sheriff observed. "Good for mosquitoes, good for a man like Karl, but you need to accept the conditions when you buy a house next to one. But he can break you in. Best firefighter in the county. Best game warden, if he ever would be."

Rupert shook hands vigorously, too, making amends for any discourtesy. "Yeah, I'll stop by. We go to the dump if you have crap to get rid of. Lots of gulls there, fighting with the crows over the banana peels. They fly a long way to eat our garbage. Up the St. Lawrence or up the Connecticut, whichever. And they eat the mice, but can't the rats, unless you shoot 'em."

Press thanked him and said yes.

"That was pretty painless," he remarked to

Carol as the squad car left. She agreed, though sorry to have been present, or spotted; commune folk wanted a low profile. On the other hand, she'd had her head in his lap beforehand, wondering whether she belonged here at all. And no, she stated, Ten Mile Farm people wouldn't have to smuggle in dope through the swamp. They had their own "Ho Chi Minh Trail," over the mountain into Canada: which was not to say she approved of it.

Press teased her by asking how else she would procure the weed she smoked, but she laughed. "Stupid question. You think we can't grow it as good as they do in the Himalayas?"

"No, I don't think that, except it's a slippery slope. Dorothy Day, your friend, is trying to help addicts, not 'enable' them."

Talking Christianity cheered her a bit and she let him kiss her, friendly-like. He helped draw out her memories of the Catholic Worker movement, not all charitable. Bedbugs inhabited the shelter, and when it was full, staff like her might have to put homeless people onto the subway for a cold night. The lectures by visiting priests and monks and the newspaper were most fun, but you rolled up your sleeves and manned, then mopped, the soup kitchen for two meals a day. Christianity was a riddle because it could be practiced so many ways: engagement, like Dorothy Day's or the Franciscans', or abstinence, like Thomas

Merton and his friend Robert Lax, whom she had actually established a philosophical correspondence with, from her cabin to his Greek isle. The rich went to church in silks, the poor in cotton, but few really thought of "the manger." Dorothy Day herself, before finding her calling, had had a daughter, who with Dorothy's blessing was also moving "back to the land," to the country, like Carol.

Press's Congregational upbringing had been pallid compared to Carol's church-window Catholicism, but he had seen it evoked in European museums. The head-in-lap episode, if he'd misinterpreted it as flirtatious instead of poignant, might have blown up in his face. She believed in sleeping with people whom you loved, and that might happen in staccato fashion after droughts, but not with Press yet. The oral incident, when he asked, had been "foreplay" to her. He trusted her, however; even trusted Rupert, and Melba, and the sheriff, and certainly his neighbors, which was progress.

"We're blessed, I guess," she said, as if to convince herself, but without confidingly snuggling up to him again. When she'd left, the Clarks called, after seeing the sheriff's cruiser go by, to invite him to a church social where Avis told him a healer was going to speak. Press was a bit amused, because he suddenly remembered Melba, on her last cleaning stint, recounting how Darryl in high school forty years ago "was always trying to get my shirt off." In a culvert that ran under Athol's main street by the garage, where she'd let him lead her if they weren't observed, alongside a trickle of brook water, he'd necked with her and handled her as he wished as long as he didn't try pulling her shirt off.

"Oh how he'd pant so! Why do men pant so? And then, with Avis, he went to a diamond store."

Avis, though not amused that Melba was now "charwoman," as she put it, three times a week for Press—"The prodigal comes home broke"—in Christian charity, forbore to nag. Avis was also genuinely kind. She sat next to Press at gospel discussions to make sure his input was included. The Clarks were like his backstop, upbeat, welcoming if he should phone or show up. Theirs was one of the half a dozen numbers he had memorized, using Information to connect him with all the others.

At this meeting the healer was a French Canadian from across the border, but charismatic nonetheless. After a heartfelt group prayer and some general Bible commentary, he progressed to the soul's influence on the trials of the body, and next separated the men from the women so each group might speak more freely. He asked each man whether he'd stayed true to his wife, and anything from the nature of his night dreams to the state of his mortgage or how often the kids called.

"Jesus had to spit in the blind man's eyes to cure him. Remember that?" he asked Press, grasping his knee to center his attention. "But Tums; too many Tums?" he intuited, and, when Press nodded, put a hand on his stomach. He wasn't healing at this session, however, but discussing Personal Balance under the title "Toss and Turn." His clinic was a big house trailer in the woods in Quebec, where you paid ten bucks to his wife for a laying-on of hands, Darryl said, who had gone there to get his hemorrhoids shrunk. They lived in an equally large house trailer nearby, and the only reason for entering Canada you needed to give at the border crossing was "The Rock," or "Laroque."

Tossing and turning was apt. That night Press did, but chewed fewer antacid pills. His hands had been squeezed by at least a dozen people unknown to him that evening; or at least, that is, whose identities he didn't know. Evanescent affection was delicious for those moments, but what was going to happen to him? A further episode of blindness, and then a nursing home for decades maybe, with world news from the BBC on the radio to keep life interesting?

Karl was now "Honorary" Fire Chief because his emphysema hampered real emergency exertion; his former duck-dog or bird-dog training clients could out-walk him, like the hunters he'd guided. So pleasures were dwindling for him too.

Blindness was like meditating at a Quaker meeting, Press decided. Other people might be present but your awareness of them was limited. In your fancy you could fill out details as you wished, or ignore them, if that felt best. When he phoned Connecticut at homework time, he'd begun to call himself Mister Magoo, until Molly or Jeremy, who laughed at first, told him to stop. Yet Carol, happening to overhear such a conversation, told her own kids, when they visited the next day, "Here we are to visit Mister Magoo." When their voices rang out from the back lawn, where the tire hung and swung, "Is that okay?" she asked Press. In case it wasn't, she gripped his hands and cupped them to her breasts. "Mama's here."

He groaned, knees buckling against her sturdiness, and she touched his hardening penis sympathetically through his pants. "We'll take care of that." But she didn't then; just cooked steaks from the fridge and frozen mixed vegetables for them.

"How's my buckaroo?" asked Melba, a day or two afterward. "Got my mop and buckets?" And, hearing her begin to scrub, he wondered, if he could have seen her, his heart would have contracted at the labor required for an old woman to earn her "macaroni money." So he didn't trouble her with his vague memory of hearing untoward sounds last night. Instead, Melba reminisced about cleaning vomit off the floors at bars after closing hours. Men were so violent, she complained. *Why* were men so violent? You had to be careful as a woman. You could get somebody's nose broken if you griped that they had pinched you or even looked at you funny. And of course that wasn't what you wanted; you just wanted to be left alone. Also, you knew that the mean son of a bitch that broke the poor jerk's nose was just getting his rocks off—didn't care about you personally. "Bothering" a woman was just his excuse to hurt somebody.

"Yeah," Press agreed. Country clubs had bullies too, although more subtle. And in the city bar you went to after trading hours, you might find out that another broker was "on a different page" in the advice he was passing to customers. Even fleecing them. On the phone to the Merrill Lynch office where he'd previously worked, he could tell he had already been reduced in status from a colleague to just another client, out of all the loops and only marginally informed.

"Men," she said. "They're okay when they're like you." And Press wondered if she meant helpless, not simply cultivated or a gentleman. "But so many times they're knuckleheads, or worse." He heard her actually start to weep, and standing up to comfort her, he couldn't find her. Was she dodging him? "I'm sorry. I had two die, you know."

Press sat down again in order not to pressure

her, but mumbled empathetically so as to accept whatever she might do; suddenly leave, or tell more of her story, or silently return to work.

"The sons want to be men like their fathers. And anyhow I couldn't afford to give them other choices. Their father was a bull rider. So I could not have told them 'Here's some money, go be a businessman.' Therefore they became a carpenter, not a lawyer or a professor. They're building ski chalets for lawyers and doctors. Not starving—so why don't they go to night school, people say? Well, they want to be a man. The father rode broncos and bulls for money in the rodeo, but at heart he was a mountain man. If he coulda *made* a living in the mountains he would have. Bulls weren't wild enough for him. I slept with lawyers and doctors in Vegas and Jackson Hole—lonely ones although not lonely enough to father a child they would have acknowledged by me. So my man was really just as good as any shyster, but then he'd go up in the snows in the mountains with the bighorns in the off-season, when there wasn't any rodeos. And he'd performed back east in Madison Square Garden in New York City, too—he was a good one! But if your boy wants to be like his father, and doesn't ride the bulls, he may climb way up into those mountains in the winter lookin' for his dad, or to be like him. And when he's lost, he dies in the snow." She choked, finishing.

After a minute, Press suggested she brew tea, if she'd like. Plus there were cookies.

"He hadn't seen his pop for a year. I didn't pick the most conscientious of men, and then I'd leave them. And I wasn't there, so I don't know if he thought his father was camping in a certain cabin up in the Absarokas somewhere or if he was just trying to get to be like him, imitate him, when he froze. They didn't find him till a month later, because he wasn't reported missing for a while. He'd been washing dishes in some joint, taking after me. And that broke my spirit. He was twenty-two. The saddest funeral you can imagine. I never got him back. So I lost two.

"No, I know men. And *why* do boys want to be like them?"

Press abstained from asking why she'd chosen macho ones, if that were the case, though you could argue that, like Rupert, cowboys had the saving grace of liking horses as she did. He also guessed that Melba enjoyed raucous, muscly, never-a-dull-moment guys. Hard-bitten had a double meaning: bitten hard by life, like her, or clamping meanly down on other people. But, as though belying his thoughts, she said, "I hope your days are good."

"If only. My eyes, you know, are like Swiss cheese, the doctor says. I see through the holes."

"I notice your hippie ladyfriend is mooching from your stuff. She eats some, throws some in the garbage."

He admitted it, grinning.

"I hear from Benny that they take their shirts off, gardening."

"I wouldn't know," Press pointed out, laughing.

"I hope they do. These busybodies harp on anything," she complained, as if on his and Carol's side.

Karl was less than satisfied with the new fire chief, his replacement, and the radio scanner brought in new titbits to crab about, as Dorothy put it. "Think about how much earlier athletes have to retire. He'll save lives. He's a good EMT—you say so yourself. That's what matters."

Karl told her that when she won the annual frying pan throw at the county fair she'd win the right to start to tell him what to do.

"That sounds scary," said Press.

"It *is* scary, believe you me. Those women will throw it twenty yards. You couldn't dodge or outrun that," said Karl.

"The pen is mightier than the sword," she answered. "Supposing I write down all your nutty ideas and hold them up for ridicule. Wouldn't that be worse?"

He admitted that it would, but then he pointed upwards because he had seduced a trio of ravens into hailing him every day as they passed over between the mountain and the swamp. Like most farmers he disliked crows, which ate your corn, but ravens were special. "Intellectuals," he called them, though they ate the gut piles hunters left, and such like.

Carol dropped in after he'd biked home from lunch.

"What are we going to do?" she asked.

"You mean 'commitment'?" he teased, in surprise. "Love, honor, and obey?"

"You want a kiss or not? Call me if you want a kiss," she said, opening and closing the front door as if once she were gone he wouldn't be able to call because she had no phone.

He gave up and got a kiss.

"You're eye candy," she granted. "But we're drifting."

"True enough. I'm a small boat. But you're raising two splendid kids very well and creating, I'm sure, beautiful art."

"A very confusing, even thorny art if it's not meant for churches, like my dad's. And I don't know what I do believe, religiously or otherwise. Or what may be quite wrong for my children. Your wife is raising Molly and Jeremy to go to Harvard, but mine are sprites—just wood sprites? My father was the best man in the world, but he had so many children he hardly knew what to do with us. Nine of us. Told me to work with glass, when I hadn't gone to theological school like him, or decided whose God to commit to."

"Well okay, do Zen glass then," Press suggested,

and she slapped him lightly, moving away. He heard her sit on the couch and adjust her skirt.

"I may be ovulating. I want to come." Yet when he started taking off his pants, "No," she added. "The other appendage that goes in and out, wiggly and warm. Oh, you are ideal. One doesn't have to do one's hair or wear a push-up bra."

"Don't marry 'em until you've wintered 'em and summered 'em, they say around here."

"Enough already from the peanut gallery. I'm not marrying anybody," she said, before obliging him, and vice versa hand job with culminating climax.

"So," he remarked, gradually recovering, meaning what next? Carol, having rested, served them juice and walked outdoors until he was afraid of hearing the brutality of her car's ignition. Her scent filled the room.

Yet she came back. "Want to go?"

Trusting meant not asking where, but he bumped into what turned out to be Benny Messer's loaner, or decoy car, also parked in the drive. When she settled him in her passenger seat she didn't fasten the straps, which signified, yes, the commune again. He was soon ensconced on the porch with curious urchins holding up fingers for him to fail to count, and toddlers climbing toward his lap. The random energies of various adults with scant ideas for what to do with themselves vibrated in the atmosphere. They brought him carrots and green salads and good bread on a plate for dinner. Then he was led inside to join many others, holding hands in a ring, the conversation ordinary except that Press didn't recognize the identity of a single one. He wondered for instance which was Jim, the guy who'd carpentered Carol's cabin for her. And had Carol vanished, abandoning him to the horde?

Then she reclaimed him, leading him outside and on a path, stopping so he could pee, till the familiar barn boards creaked underfoot. Muttering voices indicated the sleeping quarters jimmied into every cranny high and low. She placed his hands on the ladder and grasped his buttocks as a goad again. He wondered if the woman at the top had been at the dinner, scrutinizing him and eavesdropping as he spoke to his neighbors.

At the top, once more strong female fingers helped him crawl safely into her loft, then onto the pile of blankets, futons, and quilts. "Mama wants a second helping," she said, as Carol sat on the floor nearby, not playing an active role this time in disrobing him, just assuring Press that her kids were on a sleepover and they could stay all night. It was growing dark, and in surrounding apartments mildly revelrous.

She—the unnamed lady—simply drew his hands to the Paleolithic places men always have grown tumid from feeling, like the outward cradle of the hips within which a fetus will reside and her breasts that will nourish it, once born. Carol didn't kibitz this time; only lay down next to them to keep him stationary after his ejaculation so to increase the chances it would take.

Passivity was a novel pleasure. He savored it till the ladies slid apart from him and, cross-legged, chatted about factions on The Farm. The druggies, the politicals, Nixon-focused, the gardeners, the grow-your-own vegans, the social experimenters, and mate-swappers, though several had worldly ambitions beyond the commune. They were smoking weed, unwinding from the crescendo of sex, so Carol pointed out, "Potheads like us can't really complain so much, except to claim they're mercenary." Her joke referred to people who were okay growing dope commercially for the cities or running hard stuff across the border. With him listening, however, they weren't specific. A few political people would drive clear to Washington occasionally for anti-Vietnam rallies, visiting friends and maybe dropping off deliveries along the way. Quarrels sometimes evolved around them if they had more money than the others, but chipped in less to pay the annual property tax, yet might risk The Farm's future with their drug-dealing. These disharmonies so far had not split the community.

Press did spend the night, indeed, the three of them piled like puppies in the quilts, after the women produced a can for him to pee into: not to have to climb down the ladder as they did.

"So, want to take him on? He could be elected as a member," Carol laughed, in the morning, as the other woman fried eggs on her hot plate.

"No, no," Press protested, laughing too. "I'm too square."

"Twice bit, twice warned?" the lady chortled.

"Something like that." No man demanding visitation rights. The ideal dad to her, Press surmised. "Why do I need to be a member?"

"Of course you wouldn't," Carol assured him, hugging him and giggling.

"All these hippies wanting money from you to buy their uppers and downers." She and the unnamed woman then continued the merriment, gossiping about a young lady at The Farm who had just had a baby and then ate her own placenta as a mystical source of nutrition. In fact, fried it. But sure, yes, a guy like Press, whose wallet could be useful in paying bills could be voted in, "if he's a Caspar Milquetoast," as the nameless woman expressed it. Carol immediately defended him against the term.

When dropped off at home, he felt sharply wistful as Carol drove away. Why *not* live under the umbrella of rice and salads and swirling company in the kitchen instead of eventually in a "rest home," or nursing home, assisted-living facility? Well, because it really might not be so clean and simple, as some voices he heard outside that night reminded him. If it sounded like a pickup from the swamp trail being consummated, hippies from The Farm themselves might be involved. At least one druggie kid, Carol had told him, wore a pistol in an ankle holster roundabout all day. A raid with that publicity would be embarrassing to him, at a minimum: word getting back to Connecticut. *Did you hear where Press is living? Oh, gracious!*

"All God's chillun," he said to himself, hearing the voices outside again. Bystanders should be safe. Staying upstairs, he got on the phone to a night owl in New York but didn't ask for help.

Corralled by his own handicap, Press noticed Karl's increased wheeziness and irritable edge at lunchtime, when he listened to emergencies on the scanner—not to be called himself, to respond, or at how slowly and blunderingly they were being dealt with. It seemed a comfort to him to come out onto the back porch and sit with Press listening to the sweep and soundscape of the swamp. Which birds were squabbling over a speared frog— herons or ravens? A French restaurant across the border used to buy frog legs and turtle meat for their menu from him. "That could be me, fightin' with those herons for that frog," he joked. But the herons' hubbub had told him where the good frogs were, and the kingfishers, with their rattling cry, did the same for fishing holes he didn't know about, or beaver ponds newly dammed. You'd fish

77

there and then in the winter come back and trap the beaver. The bears, too, led him to berry patches he didn't know about and he'd seldom shot a bear except for a paying customer. As a houndsman, he only treed them in training his dogs. Dorothy, stimulated by Press's questions, took notes for another newspaper column, on shadbush, highbush cranberry, fire cherry, and other raccoon and ursine fare. Then there was the basswood tree, whose wood Karl used for whittling deer heads for his customers who'd shot one. Or, speaking of fire, how about "Fighting a Steeple Fire," drawn from Karl's most famous local exploit, when he'd saved the Congregational Church?

And, with the Clarks, it was amazing how a fraternal discourse could proceed for half an hour without stumbling over your fundamental disagreements about Evolution, the power of prayer, etc. Prayer certainly had a placebo effect, so why on earth argue? Whether the hay was too wet to mow was more important, though Press, after they had butchered a pig, once teased them about Jesus probably being a vegetarian.

"Where in scripture does it say that? He gave them to us for our use!"

But they understood that he was ribbing them.

Press played telephone chess with his son, relying on Jeremy's account of the chessboard, and it blossomed into some endearing moments for both of them, lovely to remember, lying in bed afterward. Feast or famine was the pendulum for him, either a banal loneliness, or richer, tender interludes mothered by Dorothy or Carol, and brothered by Karl or Darryl. The whistling dawn, the susurration of the leaves, a honking goose, and then a sentimental confab at the Solid Rock Gospel Church with a wounded soul who poured his heart out to Press precisely because he was blind and therefore harmless. Since these individuals had no money, he couldn't give them financial advice, just wholehearted sympathy. As at the commune, a toddler might scramble into his lap, and while he petted the child its mother held a cookie to its mouth and another one to his to bite and chew.

A world worth living in and for.

# Chapter 4

Alone so much too, though, he developed mild palship or antipathy toward the assorted radio personalities he spent his days with—less frustratingly than having the TV on, whose premise of presentation was that you could see whatever was going on. Some DJs were genuine gourmets about the music they played, enjoyed a passion for it, whereas others were on an ego trip. The same could be said for the variegated news commentators, right- or left-wing. Some he liked were simply women's voices, lilting or generous, inviting friendship. Others belonged to well-seasoned-sounding men, humorous and insightful about what a listener such as Press would care to know. Canada's CBC and Great Britain's BBC were refreshing alternatives, however.

But when could Carol come again? Not urgency but an incompleteness inside him asked. And it wasn't like when your wife is away; he couldn't define the lack—that muffin-gentleness she offered, pragmatic yet religion-tinged. You'd want her on your jury unless you were guilty as hell. And Carol had layers, soft yet impermeable when her confusions made her pull up short and become formidable. "What's going to happen to our kids?" she'd repeatedly said. They were being raised so differently, wood sprites versus private schooling—there must be a right way, a wrong way. "So long as yours go to college; it doesn't matter where," Press told her, which not only, he thought, was true but also carried the unspoken message that a lasting friendship with him could be useful.

Impulse was Carol's modus operandi unless a self-protective calculation intervened: is this man bad news, or the like? Her work was a governing factor as well. You couldn't be a time-waster, or derisive about learning and art. During her years at Dorothy Day's place in downtown New York she had visited the Met and the Museum of Modern Art only once or twice, and felt foolish now that her focus had changed from charity to creation and she was so isolated from such treasures, or "treasure houses." And he remembered another phrase she'd uttered once—"I have something"—that hadn't registered on him sufficiently. He'd thought she meant talent. She'd been putting off his importunities and he'd assumed this was simply impatience. Now however, suddenly he wondered whether she had been protecting him from herpes or the clap. If so he was more touched than alarmed. Indeed, she'd minimized his risk.

"So," Press teased Carol challengingly when she did show up and hugged him and let him fondle her. "I think I've figured out why you won't make piggies with me. Do you have herpes?"

She pushed him away, pausing, though not angry. "That's what your wife and you called it, isn't it, 'piggies'? How clunky, how charming! Yes, you get a blue ribbon. How smart a boy you are."

He moved to clasp her again, and when he murmured, "Thank you," she let him.

"Incidentally," he said, "when you go down to the city, do you ride with that guy—that trucker?" he asked, changing the subject.

"You mean Al, 'The Hippies' Horse,' 'The Hippie Express?'" She laughed, referring to the auctioneer Rog's younger brother and son of Rupert, Melba's friend, who hauled cattle down to the abattoirs. "Well, he hits on the women who go with him. And I'm a nice Catholic girl. I don't want to give him herpes."

"Because I thought of riding along. I want to see my kids—or visit them," he corrected himself. "And he's the quickest way out of here. He could drop me off at the railroad station in Springfield, or wherever."

She seemed startled, puzzled; he could hear her turning the notion over in her head, weighing Al's character, perhaps, and the plausibility of kindness from the strangers at an Amtrak station somewhere.

But gradually she cottoned to the idea of Al's

dependability. "He's a little different. Not a money-grubber like his brother. But how much shall I tell him you'd pay?"

He heard her lips click in a smile as she asked, which might be because he'd learned from the Swinnertons that Al charged hippie girls "a quickie" at a rest stop on the road south. But he named a modest price; then felt her tap him proprietorially on the chest. "I'll worry about you." Maybe for the first time she pronounced Claire's name, sarcastically.

Al, polite and practical, after Carol called, turned up in his cattle truck early the next auction evening, so as to meet Press before proceedings started, and to get a direct start for the slaughter-house at midnight or so.

Thus Press sat a long while on a bleacher bench listening to old TVs, sling chairs, wheelbarrows, a coyote skin, not to mention bleating calves and baying cows being laboriously sold to the highest bidder. Somebody put a beer in his hands. He had arranged for a friend to meet him on the station platform in Stamford, Connecticut, after he caught the morning train from Springfield, Massachusetts, which Al said he would easily make. The thrum of patter, spiel, and natter, or children clambering along the bleacher boards, women prompting their husbands about what to buy or pay or not, plus the ancient bray and moan of animals, biblical in tone, was fun. And Carol reappeared to take his elbow, whispering, "We need to pee outside." She'd brought her kids along to see him off and remained to ensure that Al was properly enlisted. Press wondered whether he might be growing maybe closer to hers than his own. The doomed cows obstreperously delayed the loading process, crammed in with a smattering of other herds' elderly ladies headed for hamburger but accustomed to leading their own herds to pasture. Al, though not cruel, was peremptory, having known cows all his life. "Not your best day," he informed them.

"So," he said, settling beside Press in the cab and sparking the engine to a roar, "how far are we going?" He knew, yet wanted to make clear that he was also a long-distance jockey, crossing the country a lot in moving vans, vegetable trucks, and other speedsters with a bunk behind the seat to grab some shut-eye in. "I'm divorced too," he added, to establish a link with Press's predicament. And yes, he had occasionally given Melba rides—Press's house cleaner and his dad's "reserve girlfriend."

As they hit the highway, the swarm of head-lights surreal to his diminished vision, Press blurted out a question he'd managed to stifle when he was with Melba herself. *Had* a pig eaten one of her babies?

"Well, I guess yes, to tell the truth. Hungry pig, Wyoming, wintertime. Nothing else for him to eat, and them out of the house. And nothing else, I bet, for *them* to eat but *him*."

"Rough!" they both said. Abandon that god-damned log cabin, abandon that screwball hubby. Pour soul—she had swallowed more than her fair load of grief.

Since they'd hit it off, Al told Press the slatted livestock rig belonged to him and how much interest the bank was charging. Those long-haul runs in fleet eighteen-wheelers for hourly wages were when business was slow. And he claimed to be a better businessman than Rupert, his dad. "No consignments, no wild goose chases, no hobbyhorses—like that idea people here wanted unbroken broncs from Montana. So ship in a carload that Melba finds for you!" He laughed. "Those two in their heyday! No wonder Mom's jealous."

At cruising speed the truck felt lulling like a Pullman. And the protests from the cattle jammed behind the partition lost some of its hysteria, becoming systematic, coinciding with the swaying of the vehicle, as they fought to keep their feet through each bumpy stretch. Press dozed off—it was after midnight—between bouts of asking Al questions, who needed to stay awake.

Rog, for instance, his brother, what was he like?

"Well, Rog makes more and has a pretty wife. I like Juliette. If you make more, you have a pretty wife. But people call him 'The Vulture' behind his back, the way he shows up the day after your husband dies, to see what you want to sell. That's not enviable. Me, I'm on the road. I'll pick up a runaway and be a father to her, take her to the Salvation Army."

Press, relying on his blindness to permit these personal questions, though without mentioning that he'd heard "The Hippies' Horse" pinned as a nickname on Al, asked if he didn't encounter lots of them begging for rides hereabouts or aiming for other commune strongholds like Arkansas and Oregon.

"Yeah, I sure do pick 'em up. Only they've got to tilt themselves back so two heads don't show in the windshield, in case some bastard wants to report me to the insurance company. No hitch-hikers. The license plate is all they'd need."

"And Carol?"

"Carol's a nice girl. Sure, I'll bring 'em door to door if they're as nice as her. But I've got no car seat for the children, and that *would* set the insurance agent's pants on fire."

Press asked about miscellaneous corruption in town, such as the tale of the sheriff and the airstrip supposedly used for airdrops.

"You could say a lot of things are scams. Like rich kids going to school when poor kids can't, or somebody selling stocks to people who don't know any better. Rog plays poker after the commission sales so that the farmers who sold their cattle will get home with less than they should. Dog eat dog."

"Though dogs do more than that," Press remarked. He missed his setter Flare, whom he'd left in Cos Cob for the sake of the children, Molly in particular, but would be touching soon, like her and Jeremy—anxious as to how it would turn out. Would he find a place to live nearby, or have to hire some garage guy to drive him back to Ten Mile Road? Did he even know which outcome he really wanted? And would he ever return regularly to the Big Apple to stroll the streets, or just huddle in Cos Cob hearing the lawn mowers? Al, when he asked, said that he had often crossed the George Washington Bridge, glancing toward the glittering city down the Hudson, but never ventured into it himself.

"No Christmas trees?" asked Press, mentioning Dorothy's annual trips to the metropolis with her brothers as a teen.

"No, we didn't sell that stuff, or the pies or the syrup. We didn't fuck with the tourists, cleaning their houses, washing their laundry, when they came to the country, either." But he seemed nettled at the reference to the Swinnertons, beyond disdain for the catering to rich summer people, with their duck dogs and wish for fresh cream for their morning oatmeal and maple syrup on their pancakes, served by colorful, obliging locals. Press, investigating further, found that Karl was the actual sore point, with his bossy fire-chief decisions and pronouncements and, as American Legion Post Commander, his doctrinaire concept of duty and patriotism. Al had served in the Korean War but wouldn't think of joining a veterans' organization, except for using the VA hospital for operations or checkups.

He'd seen an American soldier shoot a Korean man off his bicycle simply for fun when some civilians were passing their unit, and gotten beat up for suggesting he ought to be court-martialed. Press observed that Legion halls were mainly used for binge drinking, though Athol's was too small for a bar.

"No, not just that. I mean so many of them are ashamed of what they did in the war—killing children, maybe, and all that—spraying 'em with the sweep of the gun. They march with the flag in the parade really to try to forgive themselves and cover it up."

Press remembered hearing that drivers like Al, crossing the country, were called "Knights of the Road." But Al relaxed into complaints about rent and women, and the cattle in the back sank to their knees together as the indignities of panic subsided. Soon Vermont itself receded. He fell asleep again.

Delivered to the train station in Massachusetts, he waited an indeterminate time until the ticket master handed him to a kindly conductor who seated him in a reclining lounge-car chair, after letting him visit the restroom. He missed Carol's ministrations in that regard and mildly regretted not having questioned Al about the mysteries of the swamp below his house and the sounds therefrom. Hartford, New Haven, and Bridgeport he registered in his mind's eye. Then came Stamford, and the conductor helped him to descend to the platform, with his cane and suitcase. The train pulled out. Silence reigned.

"Press! There you are!" Footsteps and the golfer's physique and hearty voice of Roddy Wyman approached. "You look well! Those hippies up there must be taking pretty good care of you," he said congratulatorily, not of course realizing that the notion had some truth to it. "Good to see you!" Grasping Press's bag and free arm, he told him he'd "been looking into some assisted-living facilities for you, if you like them. We'd like to have you back at the club for drinks and lunch."

Roddy was referring to the country club, where you could lunch on the patio and listen to the *thock-thock* of tennis matches, whether sightless or not. He was vice president at the moment, having retired early from Wall Street after inheriting his father's seat on the Stock Exchange and finding out that leasing it to another trader was more profitable than placing his own bets or executing investments for others.

Press assured him that he'd had a fine trip and was glad to have reserved a room at the Holmewood Inn, near his former home; a groundskeeper or whoever could walk him over or Jeremy and Molly walk to him.

Roddy knew Claire and the kids—his own went to school with them—but apart from telling Press everybody was cooking with gas there, kept his news tactfully on his own family or club politics or friendly town gossip about their mutual friends. "They'll come to see you," he said. "I'll take you to the club tomorrow."

At the inn, Roddy saw him to his comfortably light-filled room and let the management know that he, Roddy, would have to be reckoned with if anything but the best of care was tendered to Press. He also saved him the embarrassment of calling Claire to announce his arrival, as well as the difficulty of dialing a few other people and cashing a check at the desk. They ordered Bloody Marys as an eye-opener. This being a school day, the children would join him for supper. Maybe tomorrow Roddy could swing by for a tour of assisted-living setups. "There aren't many," he explained, and he was relieved to be "out of the grind" himself, meaning the daily commute of sixty-five minutes to New York, even with the amenities and camaraderie of the club car on the train. "Not being generous," he promised Press, for the offer of trouble and time. But they agreed that a visit to school right now might be embarrassing for his children, before they had first seen him privately at the inn tonight. "Tomorrow, better," Roddy suggested managerially, and no, Press wasn't up for immediate reunions at the country club. "Tomorrow the club, tomorrow the school so you can talk to the teachers," Roddy concluded.

Alone on the pleasant slate terrace, Press enjoyed the complexities of a Caesar salad and another Bloody Mary—which he somewhat regretted when Claire showed up, impromptu, in case she might think he had taken to the bottle.

"I'm so glad Roddy was home to meet you. He's so obliging now that he's not trying to be his father, moving the market. Just winning the Cup every summer," she joked, referring to the club's golfing prize they'd not taken seriously themselves. "You're looking well. Color's good. They're feeding you up there?"

Press's emotions collided, both wistful and resentful. He hardly spoke but squeezed the hand that touched his. Claire said that the allergist reported that Molly seemed to have grown out of her asthma, and she was doing fine on papers in history and English, and Jeremy in math, and he'd fitted right in at "midget football." They both had friends. Enough kids nowadays had divorced parents that it wasn't a stigma.

"Yes, I believe it, and they're smart when I call. You're managing well."

91

"I hope so. It's a twenty-four-hour-a-day job."

Though registering her gripe—ironic, since she'd kicked him out—he offered her lunch, but she flapped her hand against his to say no, and responded by asking if he was thinking of relocating. Friends like Andrew or Roddy must have raised the possibility.

"Not specifically, I wanted to touch base—touch *them*. I feel irresponsible. It's been too long."

"Oh, I'm glad. They need it too. Their father. You could stay in the house if necessary. It's nice to have you close. Do you need anything we've stored?"

"What's stored was mostly for them. Pictures of ancestors I can't see, or toys they played with. I'll look at the clothes."

It was a congenial conversation; no lacerations. Yet she returned to that question of relocation. Truthfully, he couldn't answer. She asked whether he was considering selling his Ten Mile Road place.

"No, that's some kind of toehold or taproot for me, or whatever. One of the kids may meld to that bit of resource too someday as what they love and what they need."

They talked about how Jeremy loved summer camp. Rock climbing, swimming, snake-catching, sleeping out. "But it might be Molly instead who wants to recuperate from the city and teach her children about birds."

"Yes." Claire, having favored the purchase to begin with, understood what he meant. But Press also fathomed a sort of tension rising in her between a tender impulse, reaching to touch him, and reluctance or a stubborn aversion to admitting any guilt. No doubt at the club friends of his asked how he was doing, exiled to the north woods and losing his sight. This visit had not been instigated by but sprung on her, and she moved on in her choice of topics to whether she should start to hunt for a higher paying job.

"Our financial arrangements would need to be changed a good deal if you went into a facility. Quite expensive. Much more. Would you need to?"

"You mean you'd have to support yourself?" he commented sarcastically, before he bit his tongue. "No, I know, tuition," he interrupted her retort. They both said "private schools" at once. "I want that. What you don't know is that Roddy, Andrew, and some others are the ones imagining I need assisted care. I have a sort of support network so far where I am. I came down here to see my beloved kids, and go see my eye doctor, not to sue you over the settlement or spend your money!"

Claire grasped his hand to stop the argument. "Yes," she said, "and I'll send them over tonight."

"You mean they don't want to come?"

"No, no. Of course they do. Of course. They love you. They're excited."

They took breaths to calm down, and he was tired from the sleep he'd missed in the truck, on the train.

"And tomorrow you can send them off to school, and then in the afternoon."

He asked about her family, favorite in-laws, and several friends, but her hesitancy in answering such innocuous questions or telling him what time to set for supper's reservation—only perceptive to somebody who knew Claire as he did—was puzzling, till she interjected, "I want to make it easy for us, for them, you. So they don't feel they have to tell you. My friend Brad is living with us. He's moved in. Finally, this month."

Press pictured her small face. Too small—although her parents had somehow never taught her to always chew with your mouth closed. He would hear the sound at meals when her mind, in conversation, was drifting, and he had seldom brought himself to mention it. Or maybe she had done it more and more as their marriage frayed? This *Brad?* He tried to remember a Brad at the country club.

"From the club?"

"No, no. We don't go much, they're so puritan. He's in merchandising, and good with the children. They'll tell you; you can ask."

Press didn't want to hear how she had needed a man, or flesh out the portrait, so kept his trap shut, although he did wonder about Brad's finances.

Claire sighed. "I hate to hurt you. I could have written if I'd had more notice. Does somebody read your mail to you? There must be."

He didn't give her the satisfaction of a reply.

"Well, if you need assisted living, certainly you should have it. Brad has children of his own, but he could contribute to the mortgage."

"That was Roddy's idea, not mine."

"Might be a good one though." She answered his quarreling tone with a patronizing inflection; then cut herself short to grip his hands, speaking of travels in Ireland they'd shared and the jubilant births of Molly and Jeremy.

"I don't want us to flay each other. I hope you have company too. That's not what you came down here for, but to see your children—which excites them, and they need to. I'll get out of the way, if you want."

"Too painful," he muttered. She *was* a good mother. Why should they fight? The situation was a new normal. But his hand knocked over his glass of iced tea, as happened privately with some frequency, but not in front of an estranged wife, with the separation papers already signed.

Claire was touched, however, groaning in empathy. "And oh, you have spots on your pants, your shirt, because you can't see what you're eating!" She skipped round the table and kissed his scalp line, rubbing his shirt with her napkin. "If you require assistance we can change the

95

terms amenably. One forgets realities at such a distance."

She was decisive, which was nice if you agreed with the decision, even though alarmed by the speed with which she had fixed on it. But Press hadn't descended on Cos Cob seeking a nursing home. That had been Roddy's off-the-cuff, probably over-drinks inspiration, a man who had homes for everything, skiing in Aspen, snorkeling in the Caribbean, culture-vamping in Tuscany. The very curves of the roads here in Manhattan's exurbs had a comfy, manicured swing to them, he'd noticed on the drive from the Stamford train station, not like a dirt road in Vermont. You wouldn't be mistreated in this moneyed realm, as did happen occasionally in the north-woods rest homes. He'd felt more apprehensive of experiencing pangs of longing to be accepted back inside the so-familiar house, with Claire now its mainstay—of begging permission to nullify their breakup, not for love of her but to be safe again.

"Okay," they both said simultaneously. He should nap before the kids came, to be at his best and fresh. "I'll send a bag of clothes with them and you send something back for the dog to smell. I've never bad-mouthed you for a minute, you know."

He didn't believe that, since it was only human to bad-mouth an ex-spouse, but wanted to hear more about Brad. In merchandise? And not country-clubbable? Tomorrow Roddy could fill him in. And he *was* up for Molly and Jeremy's arrival, handling their heads and shoulders with welling love. To please them, he now changed into an outfit from Claire's storage room that she had folded into a shopping bag, which they remembered as a favorite from the old days. Press remembered their classmates' names and could convey wordlessly as well how much he'd been missing them. Molly told him his postcards were wedged into the corners of her mirror. Jeremy said he could throw a football farther than when Press had taught him, and once had slept out under a tree in the yard, remembering the Athol property they had begun to know during the summer before their mom and dad split up.

"It will be yours," he murmured, roughhousing ever so slightly with him. Being around Carol's children on a regular basis helped him act naturally with his despite the interruptions. He was relieved to find the stiltedness of their misfiring phone conversations were gone. And the lobster feast the inn provided was conducive to celebrating fond affections.

He asked if they preferred or not that he should visit school tomorrow and buttonhole their teachers. On the whole, no, presumably because of his handicap, although both agreed he could if it was important. Astronomy was Jeremy's brand-new enthusiasm, and he had a mentor in the science teacher, whereas Molly's circle of close friends seemed her strong point. Dancing classes loomed; would that be fun? Though piano was a bore. Ping-pong they could play at home and, unlike football, Jeremy said, didn't depend on your weight. They were white-collar children, privileged beyond Carol's—even studying French already—but somehow lent him unanticipated insights in how to talk to hers.

Brad was never mentioned, and Press bridled his curiosity. The waitress considerately allowed them unlimited time and Claire had cancelled homework supervision; whenever they walked home was okay. To their amusement, he kept sniffing their hair. It was his hair.

"Mummy said it was clean."

"It is clean. And I'm going to come to meet your favorite teachers. Just your favorites, after school. You pick them; they'll call me. No fuss; the other kids don't need to know." He thought he'd phone the headmaster on his own to register his interest and questions and presence. Stamps, coins, butterflies, and other collectibles of his youth were apparently no longer currency for kids. Jeremy had some arrowheads and signature rocks—marble, sandstone, granite, and one snitched by somebody's uncle from Antarctica— and Molly, several posters of concerts her mother had taken her to. She was half-blues, half-classical in her budding interest in music, plus pinup hunks,

Claire said. "Rock hunks," to match Jeremy's.

Press angled for specialty presents he could send them. Did Jeremy have a playable trumpet for band?

He let them go before dusk and slept long and late. Roddy had already done his morning run before talking tax shelters over Belgian waffles with Press. They went to the club then, empty except for early golfers at this hour. The tennis pro, golf-shop lady, and maître d' remembered him and the gala terrace, being prepared for a wedding party later, fetched a hubbub of memories. Roddy had planned a solo round of nine holes if Press's vision permitted him to accompany him, but the first sand trap was a hazard.

Instead, they sat with a couple of other trust funders, or proto-retirees, and talked real estate, lawn care, offspring-in-therapy, and merger mania. A message from Claire at the desk suggested he drop by now while the children were at school, and Brad perhaps out, he assumed, if he wished to. So they did, Roddy extraordinarily patient; he was a churchgoer. A new minister had invigorated St. Andrews, he said, with emphasis upon his Scottish roots, with bagpipes and the like. He muttered what Claire would probably "get" for Press's old home, before she let them in with exaggerated hugs. The layout had been changed a bit, with furniture maybe brought by his replacement. But he begged off on a tour; then

99

received an armload of clothing he could give to the inn's kitchen help if he didn't want it anymore. The dog wagged, and the shade trees, anciently formed, stirred him, and one blue spruce he'd taught Jeremy to climb and sway with in a gentle wind. These expensive roads, with Indian names—Ponus, Oenoke, Wahackme—the once-upon-a-time local chief and his two sons—and his white colonial house and hundred-year-old maples caused a pang.

Gracious, were we worthy of them? Press thought. "Buy and hold," Roddy was advising Claire, as to her portfolio of stocks. "We're in an upswing."

Press wanted to leave. "Can't you hand me off?" he said to Roddy, meaning to unburden him. But Press's impulsive hitchhike south in Al's cattle truck (which no one here knew about) had been too abrupt for him to line up a relay team of former pals who might be free to step in at short notice. They returned to the club for lunch, for want of a better idea, and the cadre of teachers would meet him afterward. Over the quiche and beet salad he missed Carol. Roddy had tucked some of his surplus assets overseas, so was speculating about the stability there. You save on taxes but could lose your principal. Socialism, nationalization, economies tanking: you had to read the *Journal* and the *Times*, as if you were still commuting on that train to the city. Japan versus

Detroit. Big Oil versus OPEC. Red China versus Singapore. New York itself was going to the dogs.

They visited on a mini-tour three assisted-living "retreats" or "villages," where seniors needn't push the envelope of their limitations to enjoy what faculties they still had. Roommates might be necessary in his price range, but they of course could be switched if friction arose. Roddy seemed astonished at what a gulf more modest means than his own could make. "Reduced circumstances," Press joked. An Ivy veneer alone wouldn't cut it, but second-tier accommodations weren't to be sneezed at, plus trips to Carnegie Hall or Yankee Stadium on a monthly docket. Each manager was glassily maternal, offering him "independent living" or "memory care," as called for; perky, entry-level voices led them to sample dormitory rooms, cottages, or suites. He and Roddy were glad to mosey on to the children's sumptuous school, where, as a trustee, Roddy had lined up more of a corps of consulting figures than Press had wanted, in order to accommodate Molly's wish for no fuss. But their conclave was not observed by many students, and did serve to assure Press that both kids were thoroughly on track, not derailed by at-home strife. Jeremy's knack for geology was intriguing to his science teacher and Molly wasn't just reading music but interpreting it on her flute. They'd both get into good prep schools, Press was told.

At the inn he fielded a few phone calls from old chums inviting him to dinner or for drinks at some point open on their calendar, which he couldn't commit to immediately because his plans were a fudge of confused yearnings. To "watch" his kids grow up; to float back to the commune with Carol; to sink into a cocoon of institutionalization. But by all means, yes, he wanted to connect with them, knowing how gossip can blossom from a single thwarted contact—*Press appears to have lost it*. One guy did alter his routine by driving over for a nightcap, after Press's children's early supper at the inn. He learned from them and him that this Brad character had older children of his own, in a "broken home" in Chappaqua, and that he seemed at least clubbable over there, marketing in a new field of technology, not IBM but parallel to it. Maybe he'd become a better partner for Claire if he married her. The children remained closemouthed on that subject but hands-on fond toward Press.

He asked them, will it be—would it be—important to you whether I live close to you in the future? They were silent, then mumbled non-committally, as if to skirt hurting his feelings or displeasure by their answers. Ambiguity was the essence of life anyhow, he realized.

"Gracious, I love you," he said. "So much, and whatever you do, whatever you want."

They collected doggie bags to take back for the

dog even before the meal ended, although it was politely leisurely; they'd gotten extensions on their homework. He described interesting people like the Swinnertons he knew in Vermont and his ride down to see them in the cattle truck, how big the swamp was, and French-speaking Quebec so near. They could visit when their French classes were over, and he would show them the Milky Way and herringbone clouds and goshawks and moose and other stuff Connecticut had lost. "We'll camp out." And then because he knew Jeremy would look up the hawk in a bird book, "Leave one 'h' out," he added.

The decision about whether to return here and stay—in fact, money was so short in Athol he could have hired Dorothy or anybody to pack up his stuff and ship it down, if he'd simply made up his mind to move into one of the "senior communities" right now—was resolving itself without having to weigh pros and cons. He took care, however, not to let slip any leanings to his children that they might blame on their time with him, except to observe, "People are kinder up there," which they would understand meant adults. "Money, money. They don't have it so they don't care about it so much, except for surviving. And for me it's all about surviving."

Quickly he lightened up. Told Molly if she wanted to sing on Broadway, she could. If Jeremy wanted to explore Outer Mongolia for its rocks and horsemen, he could. He told them he'd liked the teachers he'd met, and described his daily life up north—the neighbors, the Clarks and Swinnertons, who helped with his needs and could read any letters they wrote to him. "It's hard, having a father who is handicapped, but it's my problem, not yours, and I'm okay, believe me, please."

His nightcap later with a former golfing and club car chum, a vice president of a middling brokerage firm, was affable but odd, because it turned more on the other guy's problems than Press's. His secretary was calling him from New York here to his home, although he'd forbidden her to, and this was causing him increasing problems, convincing his wife it was for business, particularly because of the hours when she got lonely and called. He couldn't fire her because she'd threatened a suit, and the sex *was* good. But how would it end? Supposing his wife just picked up the extension phone; then he'd have a lawyer at his heels inquiring about community property. They were vultures, those lawyers. Doctors were right to want to clip their wings.

Press agreed. "Don't shit where you eat, maybe it's true," he said, repeating an old piece of clubman's advice. "Even if she puts out." Your secretary was a no-no. One guy they knew a few years ago had cheated on his wife to the point where she hanged herself. And he was shunned at the club and on the train, until, to everyone's surprise, he drove his car at a very high speed down Oenoke Avenue into an oak, fatally. This was near a place where Oenoke, Ponus, and other Indians had camped in days of yore—and Indian Rocks, on Turtleback Hill. Press had once taken Jeremy there to see and feel the holes where women had ground corn with a pestle, and you could find relic flints, arrowheads, or spear points lying around.

"What a town this is," he told the worried friend he used to trade insider tips with on the train, where nobody could hear you. Trying to think of customers he'd dealt with who had become permanent friends, he remembered a colleague who'd died of Lou Gehrig's disease alone at an expensive institution in Florida for people dying of that. He could think of customers he might have called for specialized advice, like a certain oncologist or a woman who treated autism, but not exactly a non-business pal.

"I think she's saved some proof," the guy declared, meaning his secretary.

"Probably so," Press agreed, in the Holmewood Inn's genteel bar, scented with air freshener and rather different, perhaps, from wherever the secretary hung out. "I hear the hummingbirds," he said wistfully, apropos of nothing but his house in Athol, leaving the broker at a loss for words.

*Bonkers,* the word might go out, though this was

a good guy, plus Roddy wouldn't stand for gossip of that sort, and money did talk. He explained that he had no feeder for them—only flowers in the garden—and his friend launched into a paean to canoeing at summer camp, both his own thirty years ago and now his boy's. The ogre of divorce mauled children so much, he added, referring to his worry about his secretary and his marriage, but fell silent, recalling Press's situation. Press rescued the conversation by observing that one of the pleasures of his new existence in the country was sharing a meal one day with people who didn't believe in Evolution and the next with people who did.

He couldn't continue to commandeer Molly and Jeremy away from their suppers and homework every night. Nor wrap himself in the shroud of a campus for eighty-year-olds shuffling gracefully toward the night. He couldn't work, as such, but needed to flex himself somehow in ways like work, he thought. Lacking credentials and sight he could not teach, for example. Even reading a cold-call script would be out, although he'd heard of a resourceful blind man who went to the social security office and suggested, "Give me either a job or just my damned check," and received the former, skillfully handling mediation assignments.

Doubtfully, from his room, using Information, he called a handful of widows or divorcees whom he remembered from the club but hadn't previously contacted from Vermont. Sympathetic though wary, each of them knew his story on the grapevine and didn't want to "take sides" or "be judgmental" of Claire for bailing out and divesting herself of him when the going got rough. So they were glad his call did not request that, but were cautious nonetheless about the chat, however lengthy—to be kind—lest a blind man "leech" (as he silently phrased it) onto their already touch-and-go existences. Life was complicated enough. But was he all right alone up north, they hoped, or was the call for guidance about rest homes their parents were comfortable in? He fielded soothing repartee but no luncheon invitations. They had been his "B" team anyhow to begin with, yet included a couple of voices you might enjoy hearing day in and day out. These lingered on the horn with him, as well, Lisa complaining of polishing silver in her church's sacristy for a minister less than inspiring.

"But I volunteer for hospice," she insisted. "I read them their mail and hold their hands at the end, or visit when they don't have family. We're not nurses, who do the tubes, but we're the best friend you have, who makes your calls and reads your mail."

Press, startled, answered truthfully that he himself didn't have anybody steady for that. The postmistress helped with some things, the bank teller with others, and Dorothy Swinnerton for the rest. On lined paper he could pen short replies, or sign on a dotted line where the teller he trusted pointed, but how to convey personal letters?

"Well, if you were dying I could do that for you," she teased with a tinge of distant affection. "But when they fall asleep I go home."

Those suburbs, with shrubbery where chirping sparrows nested serving as their component of nature, and nannies or au pairs from Jamaica tending to half the kids, segmented charity toward one morning a week or what was tax-advantaged. An accountant calculated the appropriate sum, which the person relegated to the opera or the Third World or whatever. A hospice visit or Red Cross phone duty was watch-your-watch because of social commitments to follow.

News of his phone calls may have prompted Claire to call the next morning and materialize for brunch, as if not to appear callous to her friends. "So what are your options? I mean the viable ones?" she asked.

His eye doctor had fitted him in for a checkup this afternoon, since Press was in town, so she offered to ferry him there.

"Well, I do have a life," he said, without of course mentioning Carol or the commune, just the Clarks and the Swinnertons. "I go to church where they believe in treating people well. They may not believe in Evolution but believe God created the Earth, so why fret about the timing? Six thousand or four billion years is not the central point if you know that every day is holy and you believe in Him."

He couldn't read her face, but more than ever suspected the silver-polisher had called and chided her. "I suppose," she said, inquiring about grocery shopping, microwaving as a solution to the dangers of the stove, oil deliveries, and the thermostat—basics of country living; that Merrill Lynch doled out his monthly allowance to the Athol bank. Yet Press was more interested in hearing Brad's history. A previous marriage and children, sure, and now he was a consultant to corporations headquartered in Stamford. A graduate of the University of Kansas at Lawrence, he was thus not immediately clubbable in Cos Cob; but should be with a little time.

Roddy and another fellow dropped in unexpectedly after a golfing date at the club, an interruption Press rather welcomed because Claire and he, while not fighting, weren't getting anywhere. Regarding the children, there was no disagreement—it was too soon for them to come visit him—nor financial concerns so far. She wasn't touching his hand this morning, maybe feeling he had ratted her out a bit to her friends, and he couldn't discern her face. Roddy, mellifluous, was a good go-between, familiar with so much, yet in the dark like Claire about Press's current life. "Do you have toilets? Do you have dentists?" he said.

"I haven't met one, but I've heard we have lawyers. Haven't been in jail for copping a feel."

They laughed, particularly Roddy's golfing mate, who was an estates, wills, and trusts attorney. Playing a morning round with wealth was simply business for him. But blindness was definitive here in the suburbs, Press realized. In the city there would be resources, sanctuaries, company, and in a Vermont village the godly evangelicals and the practical, wholehearted folk who would look after a neighbor for a more modest recompense.

"No lawyers, but they believe that monkeys were their ancestors?" the attorney asked.

"They believe different things, just like you and me, but if they believe God created the world they think the question of how long ago is secondary."

"Well, we must be leaving," said Roddy. And Claire had her usual errands to run. "Shopping, shopping," she intoned, mocking herself. "I guess all the decisions are postponed? Or, no? Are you staying a while?"

"I don't know. It's complicated. Any decision will be."

After she departed, with supper arrangements put off till later, he wandered the inn's property, his cane in one hand, stroking the manicured hedges with the other. *Free as the wind,* his mind claimed, which was true as long as you also counted its ability to fall into a depression. But free, yes, of nagging guilt that Molly and Jeremy had need of his immediate guidance and help. The outspread trees whispered privilege—the pruning by tree surgeons, injected fertilizers, trash trees culled, noisy birds excluded from nesting in them. His outlook in the past had been affluent, though made limber by two years as a draftee in the army, and the habit of actually gazing out the window at Harlem on those daily train trips. Social justice had not been his focus so much as open-mindedness.

At his appointment the ophthalmologist peered in and told him that his "SC," or serpiginous choroiditis, was about the same, though deteriorating slowly and still incurable.

The kids returned to the inn for an "aperitif," a word Claire had inaccurately taught them for the occasion so too much homework time would not be lost. They'd eaten, so they enjoyed pie during his shrimp cocktail, then left with kisses when his filet mignon arrived.

After a lonely finish, however—a weekday night was not ripe for impromptu get-togethers—he walked to the kitchen door to speak to the staff at their supper. Only a minute was required to smoke out a guy with a brother back from Vietnam, at loose ends, who would be delighted to undertake a twelve-hour round trip to the top of Vermont tomorrow, depositing him on his doorstep for two hundred dollars, plus gas.

# Chapter 5

O h, we missed you," Carol said two days after that, seeing him on his bike from her rattle-trap. "I'll stop over."

He recounted Vietnam War stories he had heard while in the car with the newly discharged and shaky vet during Dorothy's chicken-and-biscuits lunch, except then he hurried lest Carol pull into his drive before he biked back.

Of course she didn't. Impatiently he waited till the next day, when she allowed his hands every liberty in greeting her. "I missed you," she conceded, as his body spoke for itself. But she enjoyed teasing him too, this man she could pleasure so easily: starting him hardening, then stopping him. "Your wife would think you're robbing the cradle."

They laughed, both because she wasn't quite that young and Claire's opinions would work contrariwise. "You're growing a third leg. We should notify P. T. Barnum."

She went and sat down elsewhere, though. At first he couldn't make out where, but took a seat himself, as instructed, to tell her about his trip—how his mind was eased as to his kids, how Claire had roped in Brad, how hitchless the arrangements had been.

"Okay, I'm glad. Come—let's do frottage," she suggested, moving to the sofa with merciful amusement, since he had taught her the term, whereby he could lie on top of her, rubbing himself against her thigh until he creamed in his jeans. "Oh boy! Now let's get you cleaned up," she chuckled when he had. She put his pants and underpants in the laundry basket for Melba to deal with. "We're your handmaidens. You're an emir upon your return!"

He sought her lips to temper her humor, and she patted him to assure him everything was in scale. If an emir, he was a blind emir, with his wallet in her hand. "Ball in the mouth?" she teased, having told him previously that that was her ultimate test of a man's trust in her. However, it was not a proposal. She made tea and sandwiches for the porch and filled him in on gossip of The Farm. A destitute couple had shown up, and a tarp propped over poles for them, but how long would they be fed? Bald tires, no money for gas, and two foster children the state might take away from them when it found out they'd been evicted from Burlington. They wanted their checks forwarded here, as if they were just on vacation. The revolutionaries wanted to protect them, but the trust funders resented unaccounted-for expenses shouldered ultimately only by them. Besides, a state investigator nosing around might find more than the foster children.

She asked for a summary of his trip. Could Claire still rattle his cage, pull on his chain? And didn't he really prefer bankerdom? "Isn't it nicer?" Bankerdom had become her word for Press's former life.

"No, it isn't." He laughed. She laughed. "The whiskey is better and immigrants mow your lawn and corpulence is not a sign of poverty." He added that a weight was off his heart, regarding Jeremy and Molly for the time being. Carol chimed in though, with her own shifting worries about her children's upbringing in the north woods, not Connecticut. "Gramma wants them— 'Give them a proper home.' "

"So what do we do now?" Press asked, squelching a desire to propose to her.

"We do nothing. Cheer me up for heaven's sake. My life is such a mix-up."

The Clarks were pleased he had returned, having felt less certain than the Swinnertons that he would. Satan had more sway near the cities. Neither had ever visited one or left Vermont, except an apple-grafting adventure in Quebec and treatments by the healer there. "Mammon and Delilah!" he informed them, about his trip, since they could take a joke. "Those canyons of sin. No, I never went into New York, just saw my kids." He sat in their milking parlor, listening to the cows munch a ration of corn while the machines rhythmically, soothingly suckled their udders. "We each sculpt our lives," he said. "And you've done pretty well."

"Hoe your own row," echoed Darryl.

"We sure do *that*," Avis murmured ambivalently. She wanted to see Paris. Had a picture of Paris in her kitchen. Not New York or Montreal, but Paris.

"I'll bet you will, but not Germany. Will God forgive Hitler?" Press asked, seeking to stump them. But they were used to his joshing riddles. If a child-murderer repented? If you coveted your neighbor's wife but didn't act on it?

"You'll find out when you get there."

"Yet if I don't have a body, how will I feel the flames?"

"How do you feel hot or cold now? Or love and hate, dummy? Because He wants you to." Darryl laughed, having topped Press, but Avis approached and kissed him.

At the Swinnertons', he told Dorothy her biscuits seemed flakier, lighter, better. "Because you missed them," she said. She read him a column she was drafting about Hesperus, the evening star, or the morning star, bringer of light, and according to the encyclopedia, son of the dawn goddess Eos; and Prometheus, who brought fire to mankind. " 'Dusk and Dawn' is the title."

"Whopping topic. Won't you get tangled?"

"She *is* tangled," said Karl affectionately but reprovingly, having breathed too much smoke. "Creator of fire, huh?"

"And a great influence on Greek and modern civilization," she retorted.

"Well that figures."

Press rubbed Sheila the setter's ears. The rooster crowed to announce that one of his hens had just laid an egg. Some crows were mobbing an owl in the swamp from the sounds, as Karl had taught Press. It moved but they followed, which now reminded Karl of the trotlines he'd set in the river that must have hornpout rotting on the hooks, and crawfish in traps he couldn't empty. Like a man who shouldn't drive any more, he wouldn't admit his lungs' impairment, give up the hope of mucking about in the dozen square miles that had been his haunt.

"You've ate muskrat," he told Press, needling him. "You didn't know it but you did. She fried it. Delicious. You said so."

Dorothy's silence was an admission of guilt. Finally she conceded, "Once in a great while he makes me. Bobcat too."

Press smiled because he wasn't mad. "You should write a story about feeding flatlanders rats without their knowledge so they'll be prepared for the next terrible famine, when New York is under siege. Maybe the Dutch will take it back."

"This country was settled by people eating beaver," Karl asserted.

"Anyway, the mountain men in the Rockies,"

Press agreed. "And I'm glad to have. You've led an enviable life. Both of you."

"The war wasn't, but we made shift," Dorothy corrected him. Karl, however, being the type of man who would call in artillery on his own position if it would kill enough of the enemy, had sure needed her. Press wondered what the hippies would decide to live for. Not that he'd just returned from a place that had. As a customer's man, his best brokerage work was securing the old age of this clients: time for them to do what they wished.

"Yes," he said when Carol swung by to invite him on another venture to the commune, squeezing his hand as she drove. "Bring skivvies and a toothbrush," she'd instructed him, meaning an overnighter, and he'd given her what she described as a fifty-dollar bill to buy beer for the party. They stopped in the woods for a ritual pee, since she enjoyed helping him do that and had started lifting her own skirt to join in. "Our thing."

She mentioned that a new fellow had shown up from Arkansas—originally from California, but from a commune in Arkansas—who was hitting on her. "Are you trying to make me jealous?" he asked.

The farmhouse porch where he customarily creaked in a peeling rocking chair while miscellaneous children brought him objects to smell and grown-ups disputed which chores were whose felt about the same. He chewed a piece of day-old pie. Roddy and Karl, as poles, came to mind. But what should he do to be of use, talk about the five continents? He asked a boy and a girl if they could name the five, and the oceans.

"It's not school."

"No it's not. That's what makes it more fun. You don't have to be right. All the A's. America—two Americas—Asia, Australia, Antarctica, Africa. Only Europe is left out."

What to say simply came to him and they considered it. "Why the five?" came the question. "How about the Arctic?"

He explained that you subtract Australia and Antarctica if you want to be official and the Arctic had no separate land mass, only ice, but might qualify sentimentally—then needed to define officially and sentimentally. A gathering clutch of new kids had the questions and solutions posed to them triumphantly by the first two, but when he started drilling them on the multiplication tables he lost scholars.

The stippled white dots characteristic of his eye syndrome began bothering him, and he rubbed his lids.

"What's white and black?" he asked the remainders. But they couldn't guess pandas. "Moonlight" was the best answer, actually better than pandas would have been.

"What goes around the sun?" he asked. Not the moon, no. "What planets do you know?" But one had an astrological mother and aced Press himself.

"The Shaman instructs." He heard a friendly voice, calling up the memory of that woman he had twice been employed by Carol to inseminate. She sat nearby approvingly, and after a minute suggested she might be willing to give him a haircut if he wished. The kids of course wanted to watch that, and on the strength of the gentleness in her voice he consented. When she went to fetch her scissors, he regretted it, but didn't have the heart to rebuff her delight when she crouched behind him and carefully commenced to clip.

"You darling," she gushed. "I used to do this for my father, but your hair is different, and Carol will kill me if I botch it up."

The kids wanted to hear about the Big Dipper and the North Star. Which pointed to which? And how about Jesus's Star? One girl, perhaps an atheist's daughter, said there wasn't one, but Press recognized Carol's daughter Christie arguing that there was. They asked him to referee, but he begged off by claiming it happened before his time. The lady barbering him patted his head and he realized this all might be quite important to her, if she was the anonymous woman who had chosen him to father what could be her child.

Carol arrived before they reached any weepier

stage, and without betraying her friend's identity, just was amused, patting his locks. "Good job. We do coddle him, don't we?" Handing him a salad sandwich she hadn't quite finished, she asked obliquely if he needed to pee. Somebody had shot a loose moose, so there was going to be a barbeque for non-vegetarians he could look forward to. After leaving for a few minutes, she came back, saying some friends wanted to meet him. They walked a long way but he enjoyed it because their arms around each other's waists was affectionate, not just so he wouldn't stumble. The homestead sort of cabin of peeled logs chinked with forest moss that he fingered was comfortably crowded for a birthday beer party, and guys asked him how you got a job like the one he had had.

"Well, you go to college, and then you take the train down and apply. No, they don't particularly care what you majored in," he added when that was asked. "My job was to talk to people all day long on the telephone and get them to buy or sell what the research department told me was in their best interest, and I hoped it was."

"But how do you start?" a woman asked.

"You start by being interested in everything in college, not just a grind.

"And you start every day by reading the papers on the train into town so you'll know what your clients who call will be worried about. Corn futures, the Middle East."

"But why do you have to go to college," a male voice asked, "if other people do the statistics of what you ought to say and all you have to do is say it on the phone to people who don't know anything?"

Press laughed. "Just because they're rich doesn't mean they don't know anything. They can ask hard questions like you, and you'd better know which of the researchers you depend on are worth their salt—which, in a big company, you ought to believe. Besides, your customers have gone to college, or they wouldn't have the money to invest, and they may want to chat about their trip to visit the Acropolis and the Uffizi, and you'd better know where those are or they're going to ask for a different customer's man. They're lonely sometimes and want to engage with you. It doesn't necessarily matter what you majored in."

A silence indicated that he had made his point.

"And did they lose money, your clients?" Carol inquired teasingly.

"Well, not *all* of them."

"*And* you majored in?"

"History, from Garibaldi to Mike Fink."

Somebody muttered, "A bean counter," but overall he sensed he'd made a hit, and relaxed into the cowhide sling chair that had been provided for him. Dropouts were recounting tales of bad professors they'd locked horns with, or outlandish interest rates proffered by a bank on college loans. "Once you're in, it's easy though," Press remarked about Harvard. "Just show up. Why drop out?" But he knew there might be torturous reasons. A roommate had attempted suicide with a razor in their sophomore year and Press unluckily had been the one who discovered him in the process, walking in when faucets in the shared bathroom were loudly gushing and Ned already had cuts on his wrists and forehead. A gesture, yes, but Press required a week to recover his equilibrium—shook like a leaf—after his friend was hospitalized. When they left the cabin for the barbeque, hugging each other again so he wouldn't trip, he confided this memory to Carol, although choosing innocuous words because her kids had joined them.

The moose, dragged for a sizeable distance through the woods by the commune's workhorse, lay with its legs sticking into the air wildly akimbo.

"Big haul," said the guy patting the horse to the guy flourishing the rifle that had laid it low. Adding a Paleolithic note to the scene were the women who had come directly from gardening and thus were still bare-breasted, a facet Press was able to perceive. When Carol noticed him ogling them, she moved his hand from around her waist to cup her braless breasts under her T-shirt. A lot of folks who wouldn't know how to butcher a cow were suggesting procedures for dismembering the moose, and a campfire with a tripod planted over it for boiling water awaited further instruction. A pot full of moose and potato stew could be hung there, or a grill substituted if they wanted steaks—but not both at the same time—so the discussion was lively and lengthy. The hunter himself sounded exasperated about how sloppily the moose had been skinned, because they were searching for cuts of meat. No good rug would be obtainable. He'd wanted to dry and display it as a trophy, but the more dogmatic communards argued that like everything else the moose belonged to everybody.

Cross-legged as the sun set and daylight darkened, Press awaited developments. The slabs of moose meat sizzled aromatically on the fire, charring a tasty crust on the portion Carol sliced and diced for him. Someone was playing a mouth organ, and tussling accompanied the wild fare, though he couldn't recognize which kids were involved. Imperturbably the horse munched the grass. The hunter handed Press his rifle to examine, boasting that next time might be a bear. "Not this much like beef," he said, "and more for us," when the vegetarian contingent grew sarcastic about the heaps of meat.

The dancing fire, crenellated like a castle—and eavesdropping—contented him for quite a while, until when Press reached for Carol, she wasn't around. The horse was led away to pasture, kids to their homes. "What shall we do with him?" he heard someone mutter. "Bring him to the house?" A lady who told him she had trained to be a dental hygienist "in the First World" gripped his arm and led him back to his appointed chair there, after a visit to the indoor bathroom. He asked her if she wanted to look at his teeth.

She laughed. "Heavens no. Except, yes, so I can tell if you've been telling the truth. Teeth don't lie." But Press's dental work, when she peered into his mouth, looked consistent with his income level. "Lots of crowns." She squeezed his hand.

Emboldened, Press tugged her to sit down beside him and tell him her story. She acquiesced, saying she'd been an aid worker in Vietnam, doing teeth—pulling teeth because the actual dentist had too many patients—and when she came back stateside found herself living on pizzas, even cold for breakfast the next day, and so she "decided to try this."

"Is it working out for you?"

"I don't know. You tell me." She laughed. Her soldier boyfriend in Vietnam hadn't been matched, "that's for sure."

"I can be your pet rock I suppose, until you find Joe Soldier," Press suggested, since pet rocks were becoming all the rage in children's stores, Molly and Jeremy said.

"You could," she agreed, then stood up and vanished for a time. He waited for Carol also, wondering about that Arkansas guy whom she had mentioned, and realized he didn't even know this other one's name in case he needed to ask for help in getting home. But the hygienist materialized chummily again, and he asked about Vietnam.

"Oh, I loved the countryside as much as here, although it sometimes couldn't be more different. And you wanted to hug some of your patients, they were so keeled over. But it was incredibly unreal. You heard torture as you worked. And I don't mean pulling teeth. I mean they were torturing prisoners. Vietcong. 'Gooks.' We were doing that."

"You mean our side?"

"Yes, at the base nearby. We'd hear the screams. It was crazy."

"What did your boyfriend think?"

"He wanted the war to end too."

"So you wanted to try hippiedom?"

She had spent half a year of solitude at her family's in Baltimore, not even going to the movies, she said, so he reached for her hand.

"Cheating on me!" Carol exclaimed, when at last she turned up. But there wasn't much chance to thrash it out, joke or not, because he soon found himself being interviewed by a policeman, or the police," as Carol said. Was he the owner of such and such a house on Ten Mile Road?

"Yes, I am!"

"Am I correct in hearing that you are legally blind?"

"Times two," Press said to the officer or detective or whatever he was.

"Pardon?"

"I'm legally blind times two. 20/400. Legally blind's 20/200. You can call my eye doctor it you want to."

"I'd like to do that," the officer replied. "Did you know that a building of yours was being used as a stash for weed? They got it out before we got there, but there's plenty of traces on the floor. The dog went wild. Must have been hundreds of pounds."

"No. No, I didn't. No, not at all."

"Did you hear a truck? Where have you been? There are fresh truck tires."

No. Press explained that he'd been at the commune all day. He gave them his eye doctor's name and the Holmewood Inn in Cos Cob as a place he'd spent a couple of nights recently away, when shenanigans might have occurred.

Both the Swinnertons and Clarks had already vouched for him, so the police—like, gradually, Press himself now—were casting a net of suspicion for who might have exploited his vulnerability. His shed had been used, then emptied so conveniently before this raid. Carol, Melba, Al, Benny Messer, the junkyard guy, came to Press's mind, though he didn't mention any of them. He played clam except to complain about the ne'er-do-well noises from the swamp some nights.

"So why didn't you report it?" the cop asked.

"I did once. I should have again," Press agreed, but remembered how locals like Karl had told him smuggling was part of life along the border. He knew property seizure was possible in drug busts, but not if you were blind.

Yet his "pins," as he put it to himself, were knocked out from under him because were intimates of his like Carol involved, even tangentially? No, he stressed, he was not a resident at Ten Mile Farm, or a member, just a visitor; they questioned the Vietnam War aid worker sitting next to him more than Carol because of her proximity. At least it wasn't hard drugs, and they hadn't gone to Carol's cabin or their dog would have found marijuana. But what a coincidence, for her to have brought him here just when the shed needed emptying!

They had no warrant to search the commune, just his own place and of course had found nothing to incriminate him, not even butts left by Carol. Ten Mile Farm had sounded unusually thinly populated as the cops circulated; probably a good deal of pot was being destroyed off-site.

People's main concern had become who might have tipped off the dealers ahead of the raid, which in a sense was Press's also. Who was a dealer? Who was a snitch? Hadn't Carol turned up unexpectedly this morning to scoop him out of there? Had all her visits to him been motivated by measly thoughts? No, of course not—and yet? Ouch.

He squeezed the hand of this strange Vietnam-vet lady, who muttered with amusement, "Uniforms." Odds on, at least he wouldn't hear intruders around tonight. He kissed her slender hand without a peep from Carol, wondering if maybe he could stay a while.

"I'm a very well-behaved blind man," he promised.

"If I ever need one I'll remember that," she teased back. "You forget I've been in a war zone. I've seen men with their legs blown off waiting to be evacuated. I saw our Vietnamese torture Vietcong they caught by tying a phone wire to their penises and cranking the battery handle it ran to. Or they'd put them in a cage, all woven of barbed wire, so small they couldn't lie or stand, for days in the sun. But I didn't try to save them for fear my orphans would suffer if I was thrown into a helicopter and shipped out."

Press, without calculating how to respond, laid his head comfortingly against her shoulder. "I'm sorry," he said, and she put her fingers he wasn't squeezing into his hair.

"So if this zoo doesn't hit the sweet spot, where should I try? Maybe Bangkok again, or Beirut, or

Bangalore? Anywhere there's no spooks and no paratroopers. I'm not amused anymore by spooks or paratroopers."

"But won't you miss the rush?"

"No. And I'm going to lose my security clearance anyhow for staying here." A college classmate had inveigled her into noodling here awhile and chilling out. Hash she didn't use, having had her fill in Vietnam; nor bullying, weepy men strafing "gooks" from the air. "But if you are a pet rock, can I pick you up and put you down?" She shrugged the shoulder he was leaning on to free herself.

"Sure. I'd like a break. I'm forty-six, so the undertow is beginning to get to me."

"Then what are you good for?" she asked, in a kind tone.

"Oh, a man around the house has his uses. A dildo; an ear to talk to; two arms around you; a voice from the next room when you're lonesome."

"I have a dog to talk to."

"That might be a deal killer." For the umpteenth time he squeezed her hand, signaling that if a pet rock was needed, "Barcus was willing." Carol was lanky, this one seemed short, but where was Carol? It would be a mistake to poison their friendship with jealous suspicions when Carol was way past the toying-with-him stage. He could end up stranded.

He inquired about flings and she told him a West

Point graduate had flown her to Tokyo for R&R. When he asked if danger had added a frisson to sex in Vietnam, she said, "Do you mean like doing it with a man who's going blind? There are lots of people around here or anywhere to feel sorry for, so you don't sleep with a twenty-year-old kid who is shitting his pants he's so scared, or the stockbroker who wonders what life has in store next. We have that in common. But do you feel sorry for me?"

"I'm ready to," he promised jokingly. "Easy does it. If you were prettier you'd be eye candy."

He felt a tap on the shoulder and realized Carol was ready to drive him home. Who else, indeed, would have?

"Your harem," she said, but her kids were with her, so no more. "Jim wanted to talk to me, and this other chap from Arkansas. I'd like you to meet him."

# Chapter 6

P ress sank into his squeaky porch swing, alone, and listened to the evening birds. The trees, though not protection, were comrades, he thought, rooted where they were and couldn't leave, had to face the music along with him: fire or windstorm. Eating cottage cheese and peanut butter from their containers with a spoon, he contemplated his situation. Probably safer than before the police raid and maybe no more lonely, unless the Clarks and their Solid Rock Gospel congregation stopped making allowances for the rumors of his consorting with free-loving, drug-snorting souls. But the Clarks always spoke of Carol, like Melba, as a cleaner, charwoman, and eyesight aid and his hosting her children at his house as perhaps a kindness. At church, more than once, families ambitious for their children's future had introduced Press to them so he could talk about what college was like, how to prepare for it, and what it could do for you. A few Sunday dinners he'd been brought home for had been devoted to what the parents hoped were pep talks or verbal quizzes that might boost a high school kid toward glimpsing what college conversations were about. Maybe Carol was similarly forward-thinking.

Out of loneliness he phoned Dorothy and Karl to

apologize for missing lunch that day without calling. "So who—whose pot was stored in my shed, and who ratted them out to the cops, and who tipped off the drugsters?"

Karl laughed because town-wide gossip had it that "all three or none" could be from the Sheriff's Department itself. "Like with soldiers, your best fighting men can be hell-raisers on leave. Your bravest fireman or deputy might not be Emily Post when the fire's over. I've seen them steal stuff right from the embers."

"And how about hippies?"

"Well, you know the hippies better than me, but aren't they just users and retailers? This seems above their pay grade, and they don't speak Italian. When you are counting the money, in Canada you want to speak French and in New York it's better to know Sicilian."

Press appreciated the humor to demystify the incident, though he thought more of the potential for good or evil of the hippies than Karl. You didn't need to be Italian to shuttle drugs back to your old neighborhood in Brooklyn, particularly if you were already selling Vermont pistols to a street gang as well, like the guy who had given Carol her case of herpes. Nor did you have to be a Frenchman to make mischief in Montreal.

Next morning Press, after the BBC and Canadian news programs, biked to the Clarks' in time for milking, to touch base with other friends again, as Avis immediately recognized. "Hard for you! Here in the boonies. We're not used to it either. You used to know your neighbors, so if they were running rum it wasn't scary and you didn't tattle and they made their separate peace with the law and the Lord."

She brought him a three-legged stool to perch on while listening to the cows munch their corn or cuds and the machines rhythmically pump. He could even hear the barn cats lap from their bowl and skirmish sveltely with each other. "You're in the clear. They won't be back," she assured Press.

Nevertheless, at midday a detective did drop by for a further chat. "Hope we didn't disturb anything when we searched. I should think, though, you might have an idea who was doing that, in retrospect. We've checked you out in Connecticut and all that. You were not responsible, but thinking back, you must suspect somebody."

Press didn't give up Carol's name, of course, or implicate Ten Mile Farm, but when he answered that, being a newbie here, he didn't know, the other man mentioned both her and Melba. Press then pointed out that a hiker's and hunter's trail led people into his yard if they were in the swamp, so he often heard voices he had no explanation for.

"Well now it's different. Call us," said the cop.

Melba arrived to houseclean before Press's depression about the visit had cleared, and sped that process along.

"They got nothing on you. No judge would blame a blind man." Al, Rog, Rupert, and she also appeared cleared of suspicion after short interviews. "So get on with your life. Figure it's like living next to a big auto dealer who's making tons of money and you're not. So what? Forget it."

He realized she meant the swamp was like a dealership. People sometimes made piles of money off it, but don't eat your heart out envying them. To his silence, she went on with the subject. Long-distance truckers had the choice—or even snowbirds returning north in their cars after wintering in Florida—of running a delivery as a mule for the mob if they had the connections. "If you bet the rest of your life you can wind up with a lotta money."

"Yeah but how do you meet these folks?"

"Well, mainly through me because I was in Vegas so much. But you're dead if you don't deliver."

Press looked startled, even guffawed.

"No, no not me. I was a bed-maker, and my guys didn't do Horse. They rode broncs and bulls."

He laughed because her scope as a motel bed-maker had been so inclusive.

"Are you stumped? You think a wise guy hides his piece when the maid walks in the room? A girl's gotta work. I had my babies to feed. And you're sitting pretty. Why is anybody going to bother you? The cops know you're blind and so do the bad guys. You've got money coming in but not too much."

"A dribble. Lucky," Press agreed. Since Melba then seemed more interested in who'd ratted out the dealers to the cops than the crooks themselves, he slipped into his separate musings. Was he Carol's "pet rock"? And didn't those innumerable hours she devoted to cutting and fitting together stained-glass mosaics, plus her love for her kids, argue against his unease that she might have suddenly appeared and whisked him away from his place yesterday for a purpose? Wasn't it really a coincidence? Though she was a pothead, to use the vulgar term, surely only a consumer, not a dealer? Why chance going to jail, where you couldn't jigsaw lovely colors and designs, or hug your children till your time was up? Yet what about her *wasn't* illogical?

"Play it as it lays," he murmured to himself.

"Amen," said Melba, kissing the top of his head in passing, with her pail and mop. A woodpecker rapped, and he hoped that might be enough company after she left. She wanted to go home and nuzzle her horses.

He'd called Jeremy and Molly last evening and did so to touch base again when school let out, though not saying why. Also he went through his drawers and closets to settle his belongings in order again after the police search. His little cache of household money for paying Melba, buying groceries, etc. had been discovered but not disturbed. He walked around the shed where the pot had been stored, while listening to a pileated woodpecker holler in the swamp; then tuned in to a French-language classical music station to reclaim his downstairs for himself. No cops or crooks. But by nightfall, getting lonely again, he called the Clarks to see if any church socials were planned, and Roddy back in Cos Cob, to thank him for his help, but really to talk. Roddy was out, and though his wife was polite to Press, one needn't envy their round of activities to wish more for oneself. He missed the whisk of Melba's broom, and anticipating Carol's next visit, wondered why these were becoming few and far between. Would he grow bats in his belfry— flap, flap? He wished he were blind like a bat. Echolocation would be marvelous.

He slept past dawn with milling personalities in high-key, bossy dreams. Then a Sousa march woke him from his gnomish radio, and outside an animal nibbled birdseed under his window. It was hard to believe, when roused from such a rich harvest of dreams, that he was blind. So impoverishing. He saw daylight and bipedal forms, tree crowns and running water. But was this the place for him to live?

"I wanted to see my friends," Carol said, driving up when the sun was high and hottish. He'd just returned from a wordless lunch at the Swinnertons', gloomy because of Karl's wheezy emphysema. The labored breathing, plus his nose hook-up to a cylinder of oxygen, depressed everybody. Press wondered whether Karl's lung problems weren't more dire than the cursory clinic diagnosis.

Carol led him to adjoining chairs, fetched a brush, loosened her hair, and told him to attend to it. When eventually he finished that task they stood and hugged. She felt him harden against her thigh. "Oh, that's another friend. And he probably wants some attention."

Letting well enough alone, Press didn't answer while luxuriating in playing with her breasts and bottom and received a considerate hand job.

Since they both were still panting just a bit, she waited a couple of minutes to explain her actions vis-à-vis the drug raid. "Luckily I was home. A guy showed up out of nowhere and told me, 'Get him out of there!' I'm not going to say who it was or if I knew him."

Press also wanted to know if she'd been less directly aware of what was going on on his property, but let that ride while he returned to attending to her waist-length hair. Carol herself used only her fingers to untangle and pile it up, then scissors before it reached down to her coccyx.

"I promise you, I'm sorry. It's what I don't like," she said.

"You mean smoking dope?" he asked sarcastically. "How's it get to you otherwise though? You can grow it here, but in the city?"

"I know my inconsistencies." Jerking her head away, she moved out of reach.

"Prisoner's Base," he said, reminded of the children's game in one version of which you had to touch the blind-folded prisoner at "prisoner's base," a certain tree, or whatever it might be, and he *was* a prisoner. This softened her. Fathoming his meaning she moved a little back.

"When you were handling millions in other people's money, you must have seen things done you wouldn't have done yourself?"

They laughed but found nothing to talk about. She wouldn't let him pet her hair, pinned it up instead. "I overlook *your* wicked ways. My dad doesn't like pot at all either, that's for sure, but I suspect he likes Wall Street even less. It's called the Catholic Worker movement, that he and I were in, or elsewhere, Liberation Theology."

Press considered this notion of equivalence seriously, maybe for the first time, although Carol had joked with him before about being regarded as "a pig" in the canon of younger people of her stripe. "If you weren't blind I wouldn't touch you with a ten-foot pole," she'd joked previously, but now claimed flatly, "In a better world, what people like you are doing may be illegal and what I do may actually not be."

Though silent for a while, she radiated first impatience, then patience again. "You know," she stressed at last, "If you think about it, your safety has always been my concern. Not infecting you with herpes. Not letting you stumble and fall; or starve from loneliness; or get caught in any cross fire from this. I had very little knowledge but was looking out for you."

"I believe you," he replied untruthfully, yet stretched out to touch her even so, as she stayed out of reach. "Don't leave." He could see her shape straying toward the porch.

"No. I can understand your viewpoint. Shall we run away together?" She laughed. "Wouldn't that be scarier than my suing you for palimony?" She moved to his side, however, and placed his hand inside her thigh. "Don't be scared. We're not ogres, us potheads, and I hate the hard stuff. Are you a leg man or a breast man? Shall we test?" she teased.

Press was at a loss for words. "I do think we could test you, some time when you're up to it. Touching different parts of my body. Seeing how hard you get."

"You win," he told her huskily, as she ran a sort of preliminary examination along those lines, meaning his suspicions were trumped.

"Then sculpt me," she reiterated, harking back to her script for tantalizing him after they met when he climbed Jack Brook. "Better yet, I've brought you a Barbie doll one of my friend's kids outgrew." She took it from a bag and put it in his hands. "You can finger her." And she kissed him to lighten the import of leaving him with Barbie's boobs.

What do you do about claustrophobia? In jail, he figured, there might be no evading the panic except to live each day for itself with a few make-shift, shaky alliances stitched to other jailbirds. He had his ears, feet, freedom, and judgment, a telephone to connect to his memories, a melodious voiced, high-collared bank teller to read his mail to him, and had solved the problem of reading numbers on his greenbacks by carrying a wad of fivers in his left pocket and ones in the other. And he'd sit on the steps of the Memorial Building listening to the town's bustle around him, if he wasn't accompanying Karl to the pharmacy, or slowly pushing Dorothy's cart at the supermarket. So life seldom seemed not worth living when he flexed his blood into circulation in bed in the morning.

Carol dropped by two days later, asking if he wanted a ride to town for shopping. Wordlessly he got in the car, and from the post office crossed to the bank to have that favorite teller help with his mail as usual, cutting Carol out of the process. In the food market, though, she retrieved hummus, V8 juice, raisin bread and raisin bran, pitless olives and olive oil, yogurt and cottage cheese, bananas, Thousand Island salad dressing and greens, and a roasted chicken for him.

"I don't know what to do," he said. "Stay on Ten Mile Road, or scram, clear out. What do you suggest?"

"Well, that damned drug bust. Can't you forget it? As you know, I've often said we don't like— my friends and I—the drug stuff for money."

Press sighed. "Okay."

"No. You must be enthusiastic," she decided. "I won't let you starve, but I won't be your friend unless you adore me." Letting him off then, she laughed while he protested that he did adore her. She lingered like an angler with a fishing pole before driving away.

Whatever the truth, he figured that being downtown with Carol after the police raid might implicate him a little more in the suspicions of locals like his Solid Rock Gospel friends.

He did receive another police visit, a detective asking about recriminations, echoes, second thoughts, night movements. He heard the fellow search around the cellar, attic, and outside. "I think I'd be an unconvincing witness in court, nearly blind," Press suggested. "This trail in the swamp goes back to rum-running in Calvin Coolidge's era, probably to the Underground Railroad, if you know what that is."

"I know more than you think," the lawman replied, so Press apologized for sounding sarcastic.

"No, it's scary. Hey, please, I want you to catch them, hippies, Mafia, or rednecks, whatever they are."

Melba's noisily unregistered car arrived, fortunately after the cop had left. "Gobbledygook," she announced, to dispose of the fuss. "Those peaceniks." Her casual chaffing made Press feel better about the situation. "They've looked at your bank records, I assume. You're all clean, though those druggies ought to have paid you. Storage space," she chuckled. "People like you who were born with a silver spoon in their mouth are always safer. I bailed out plenty of boyfriends in cow country, and yet, all told, even scrubbing your deck, I've never been sorry I left."

He didn't mention the son dead in the snows of Wyoming's mountains, or the horrible story of a baby eaten by pigs in the homestead cabin, since that would have been like asking if Melba was sorry she'd ever lived. His own scenic memories included Rome's Capitoline and Janiculum hills and the Borghese Gardens, honeymooning with Claire, doing the tour. "Old and new," he said, meaning where their exploratory tastes had taken them.

"God is so cruel," she murmured reflectively, as though answering him.

"Yes," he admitted, from the vantage point of going blind. "Though maybe people are kinder if He made them that way."

"You've run with a different crowd. Rich people are nicer to rich people."

"Sure. Yes. That's why I've washed up here. Rich people couldn't have been nicer to me."

She laughed with him. "Well, nicer than to a charwoman, anyhow."

"Probably so. I bet you had fun in your life, though. Those cowboys with their heads in your lap after they'd won a silver belt or whatever, all busted up."

"I'm pretty particular about my lap. It's like a wrangler may be breaking broncs for a living, but he'll have a love-horse, a horse he loves. I'll cook his oatmeal for him, when he's left his teeth out there in the ring on the ground, but if he don't have a love-horse too, that's all. You know a man by his horse and by his dog."

"I'll bet," Press agreed yet again. Silence followed, except for the flop of the mop, until she opened up after a few minutes to tell a funny story she'd been recalling lately, "because you can't do it over." She'd once hit the road alone after a disappointment in love—being dumped or dumping someone herself, and before she had kids. Leaving a ranch near Elko, Nevada, she drove to Reno, then up the Sierras to Truckee and down the California side to Sacramento, where she decided to skip San Francisco and headed instead for Point Reyes, up the coast, for some good beach time.

"I had my tent but it was too cold to swim. There was driftwood, so I had a fire. Deserted beach, seals barking—I could unwind—except along came this guy after a little while, which I didn't want at all if he was going to hit on me. But no, not a creep; he didn't stop, walked past, quite aloof. Then, uh-oh, he turns, comes back, yet hardly looks at me. He looked off as if at someone else. Hands me something. 'Don't want to waste it,' he says absently, as if a thought, not very important, had popped into his head, and walked on. I didn't even notice what it was for a minute, I was so puzzled. Of course it was his wallet. And he drowned himself after he got out of sight."

"Ouch. Awful."

"Could I have helped? And afterward I didn't give it to the police for his family or talk to them," she added, interrupting his assurances. "I moved my camp before the sun set, even before I knew what must have happened, and then read about it in San Francisco when his body washed up."

He said nothing, though wanting to know how much money had been in the wallet, till her silence prompted him to assure her again that she couldn't have saved the man. "And who would want all those interviews?"

"No, we don't do interviews. Buckaroo wives. They only talk to you when you're on top. If your guy breaks his ass and there's no news guy around.

"You're a square," she told him, approvingly. "Have you ever broken a bone? Have you ever been in a fight?" When he shook his head, "That's the spirit!" she hollered. "So many men, when they get tanked they want to slug somebody. Get a hard-on and want to push you down. Ever even been slapped?"

"No. But you liked the bad boys," he teased. "Not us good boys." He felt her chapped or wooden lips brush his cheek as she passed.

"Well, they're more touching. Nothing ventured, nothing gained. Till they're knocked flat."

"Then you pick them up," he laughed, finishing her thought—but tried to think of anything he'd ventured, beyond joining Merrill Lynch and marrying Claire.

"But not the grabby guys like Rupert and Rog, with dollar signs for eyes and bank accounts like you. Like you, only mean," she added, lest he feel offended.

"Grabby guys are charmless," he agreed. "I've known a lot. But Rupert is your oldest friend, is he not?"

"He's been known to get into my pants on occasion, yes. Is that how you define 'oldest friend?'" She chuckled.

"Your call, not mine."

"Rupert was a business partner, not someone I would have fallen for, after high school. I shipped horses to him and seldom got my money back."

"And yet you're living in his trailer? Is that sad?"

"Yes, I am. He took me in to spite his wife and drink tea with, honcho-wise. Men like playing padrone, but he's not as bad as they come."

"You had no crooks?"

She snorted. "There were girls who liked the dudes that would sucker punch another chump in the solar plexus for no reason and go home with him. They're the ones you read about who go to prison for driving the getaway. I'm the type who'd pick up the guy who couldn't catch his breath."

"The Good Samaritan. St. Peter will wave you right on through."

"Oh, no, no. A blind man gave me a C-note once for a tip, thinking it was a ten, and I never told him."

"Not *me!*"

Having forgotten Press was blind—though his presence might have prompted the memory—she spryly hopped in his lap and hugged him.

"You're as light as a feather, you should eat more. Listen, if you ever find me dead, search the house before you call the cops because I've hidden money around and I want you to have it."

Melba, at a loss for words, stood up and lectured him about how stupid that was if the police had found it to prove he was in with the traffickers. "But sure, hey, give it to me now and I'll be sure to give it to your hippie girlfriend then. Hasn't she already found it herself?"

"I'm not guessing who's found what, but I wish you weighed more than ninety-five pounds. I'll give you a twenty for ice cream."

"I'll take it. That's two hours' work. But I can't promise I won't pay my dentist for the last tooth he pulled. So the frog skins are so you can get out of Dodge?"

"I want to be able to. Flag down a car. 'Take me to Montreal.'"

"You're blind, but, sure, with a nice guy you'd get there. Then what?"

"The kindness of strangers. It really does work. Just like here." He laughed.

"Yeah, Al and me are kind. And Avis Clark, if you didn't get in her husband's pants before she did. And that newspaper lady who takes your money to feed you. But they'd deport you back."

"Then I'd get on the New York bus," he joked.

"And then you'd be fucked. Real sorry you weren't back here."

"Right you probably are. I'm stuck." Yet she was chopping kindling for the birch log in his woodstove, so he felt less stuck. The wave of warmth that followed was luscious, whereupon Melba rehearsed with Press how to find an exit in case of fire, checking, for example, that all of the likely windows could be opened with a push.

"I need to know," he blurted, to his surprise.

Melba took what she described as a twenty from him. "Enjoy yourself," she repeated after hearing him sigh. "That hippie that gives you head—okay, she's got two nice kids—and if your wife won't let you see your children, enjoy *her* children. That's what I mean. You're quite lucky."

"Yes," Press conceded. "God bless you. Don't leave. I may be lucky but I'm lonesome too."

"Don't be afraid of the dark." She tousled his hair tolerantly. "I've never known a man who wasn't scared of more things than I was."

# Chapter 7

That night, sleeping soundly, Press was awoken by the wail of sirens, suddenly throwing him back to his city days. They went toward Karl's place or Benny "Bear" Messer's: he of the spyglasses, and rassling the boulders out of Press's spring. However they shrieked back rather soon, maybe from a disaster at the commune. Thus an ambulance, not cops or a fire truck. He resisted calling Dorothy's house until daylight, even though the noise couldn't have failed to wake them too, not to mention the scanner that Karl kept on all night. Ten Mile Farm's medley of loose-cannon characters made any accident possible. Busted backs, a bloody miscarriage, a gun going off. At sunrise he called the Swinnertons to check on their welfare.

"No, Karl's not okay," Dorothy said grievingly. Press offered to bike over and hold the fort, since she was going back to the hospital "in a minute," and by the time he'd done so the house was his. Sheila, the setter, welcomed him with nosey requests to be petted and he found day-old doughnuts in the bread box and coffee on the stove. Dorothy had let the chickens out, so they must have been fed, and the cats as well, both barn and house. He answered the phone when friends called for information, but knew less than they did, being unable to dial the hospital. Apparently the emphysema and bum heart had got the best of Karl overnight, but the EMTs and ER folks had stabilized him.

Press moved from kitchen chair to parlor sofa, out to a porch rocker and back to the settee. Missing his friends, he wondered whether Karl was suffering even if out of the woods. Nothing could be worse than struggling to breathe; another friend had died last year gasping from Lou Gehrig's disease. And when was their tax bill due? He'd thought of adding a few acres to his holdings to help with their arrears. Not stinginess but uncertainty about his plans to move or stay had delayed him. But his own unease and discomfiture shriveled by comparison with what they must be feeling. Firemen buddies and the Legion commander all called, and he groomed Sheila, washed a few dishes in the sink, and listened to the two roosters announce individual egg-laying by their respective harems. Shamefully, it occurred to him that if Karl didn't survive Dorothy might take him in as a permanent border. "Star boarder" was a country term for a boardinghouse resident who shared his landlady's bed on cold winter nights and sweaty ones too. It was a comfier house than his own.

He was watching TV when Dorothy called to say that Karl should be home in a day or two and therefore relieved him of duty, and sinful fantasies, in the meantime. He lingered, savoring the pleasure of a house not his own, putting water and feed out for the cats, and chickens, scratching the chest of the dog. Then, wobbling home, he was surprised when a pickup stopped to offer him a lift. Who was it? Couldn't see; farm trucks resembled hippie trucks, except for the faces, unless you could distinguish what lay in back. He sniffed for fertilizer, hay, or manure.

"Want to go to Ten Mile, bro, or back home? I noticed you," said a male voice, youngish, most likely a hipster's. Press, being lonely anyhow under the circumstances, impulsively chose the commune. He felt the truck turn around, then wind uphill on familiar curves to the same creaky porch and, after somebody was shooed out of his cushioned chair, settled there.

Before gunning away, the guy sat on the floor next to him, and turned out to be Carol's friend from Arkansas.

"I was thinkin'. I go to Portland regularly for fish. Would you like a ride?"

"For fish?"

"Yeah, I do a run for the stores. Lobsters, fish, et cetera."

"Maybe I would." He patted Press on the shoulder like a pal before he left.

Nobody else welcomed or rebuffed Press. Was he now a garden ornament? Would Carol be summoned, or an acquaintance lead him to their quarters? Conspiratorial notions simmered in his head—how long would he be gone from his house and what might happen in the interval? Common sense, though, returned as he realized the absence of children must be due to school, and a house like his would seem radioactive to a bad apple immediately after a police raid. Maybe the communards felt a bit guilty, or were simply busy with their lives? A woman did touch his knee and ask whether he needed anything, but moved on without hinting if she knew him. He might have asked for the woman whose loft he had climbed to, except she had purposely withheld her name. The shape of the barn was visible to him, but to go and search for that ladder, after finding the entrance, would be dangerous, or folly even should she be there.

The buzz of a nearby beehive soothed him, plus the merry-go-round of residents stepping in and out of the farmhouse to use the phone, put a tape in the boom box, or perhaps carry fixings for the next meal. Honey, he remembered hearing, was part of The Farm's self-sustenance program, like maple syrup, banty eggs, or leather goods that they sometimes sold. The bees hummed industriously in the flora around the porch and barn swallows hawked for bugs overhead: *kvik-kvik*. Somebody handed him a vine-fresh tomato to eat with his hands. It dripped in his lap, so he asked them to lead him inside.

While there, he had this person help him to call Dorothy to make sure she'd gotten home when she expected to and if her morale was up. A friend had joined her to drive her back and forth since Karl was going to be held over. His mood was cranky; didn't want bypass surgery. "No knife!" She'd be at the hospital tonight. Certainly he could come over tomorrow and feed the animals. She sounded like she'd been crying, but with her many friendships and his handicap, he knew a more complicated offer of help would be unwelcome. Some communards, overhearing his conversation, invited him to hold hands around the dinner table in silent meditation and partake of rice, salad, and pie. The talk was affectionate, with children there, about Karl's ambulance ride—a man they knew to be Press's friend, who had helped so many people as fire chief or into that ambulance for their own last ride.

"Does Carol know you're here?" a person asked, and Press said maybe not, if nobody had notified her, which he knew was hard to do. "I'll give you a ride," she replied, but they left it at that till the light waned outside, supper was over, the kids urged toward bed, and new people had shown up, with a guitar. He smelled marijuana, but "in deference to you," the lady said, nobody was dropping acid or using mescaline. Press

153

grooved to the guitar, especially when it was backed up by a Credence Clearwater or Jefferson Airplane tape. Eventually his interlocutor tapped his shoulder and led him to her car, seated him next to her, tied the bike to the trunk, and drove him home. Didn't ask where, or whether he wanted to go to Carol's instead; just said, "Come any time." Then asked, "What's it like to be blind? Stupid question, hey?"

"No, but hard to answer, which means it's a good question. Ups and downs. Kind people. This is an up."

She fobbed off his own queries except to confirm that she was a chum of Carol's as well as the guy who had picked him up. "Join if you want. We know you by now," she joked, after delivering him, hand on elbow, to the door. "Do you want me to walk you through your house?"

"No, sweetie. No sweat. Best of luck."

He didn't so much as know who she was to ask after her someday. Yet yes, as he'd said, it was an "up" on a down day, and he wasted no time before phoning the Swinnertons, which yielded no answers before bed.

Next morning Dorothy took him along on her breakfast visit to the hospital. Karl was gruff and grateful, stoic and self-pitying, like any other patient. The murmurous scents evoked memories almost prenatal in their blurry scope. It pained him to remember conversing with his dying dad, a colon tumor having metastasized, ungracefully though sympathetically agreeing with him that at just sixty-three he had already seen the best of the world. He also recalled the births of his children and tonsillitis, appendicitis in his youth.

As to Karl, though fond and rooting for him to pull through, Press felt he wasn't moved enough. Dorothy tried to cheer him up, drawing out otter lore, duck dog lore for a pretend column. He changed the subject to fires, what you breathed and what it did to you, and how far, if you passed out, you'd fall. One barn had burned with all the cows alive inside, pinned in their stanchions. Their bawling tore at your heart, and the farmer had gone so crazy he started shooting them before they died more painfully, thus endangering the firemen. Then at Anzio, that dud German .88 shell rolling into his foxhole. A nurse interrupted, lest he become over-stimulated.

Press, on her porch, agreed that he wouldn't be the same with an oxygen tank to drag around and tubes in his nose. He walked home for the simple pleasure of exercise, as Dorothy's agitation segued into a wish for privacy. The leaves were tinged with colors, and nattered even when he couldn't see them, the sky shortening its hold on daylight, birds flocking with migratory calls. He thought of Jeremy and Molly: how to connect more with them this school year. Easy improvisations like having them mail their history and

English papers wouldn't work; nor reading them to him, which anyway he might like, but not them. Mentors were everything in education, but you only knew that later, so he should encourage their ties to favorite teachers in any subject. What you looked back on was the stance, the courage or humility of sixth grade, eighth grade, high school teachers. "Know who your friends are," one had said to Press, a wiser adage than he'd realized at first. Not just to protect yourself, but to protect *them* sometimes from the cruelty of your own arrogance when speaking to people you knew would overlook or forgive your thoughtlessness. And reading was traveling he must tell them; reading is hitting the road. Molly could play the piano for him, and if he delved deeper into his memory he could unearth more stories of his family and himself to tell.

The slatted sunlight on the splintery floor was lovely and the scent of bats, or birds, skunks, coons that sheltered in the defunct barn seemed an olfactory carnival. A porcupine, interrupted by him as it gnawed on a salty board, shook its greeny-white quills. Press retreated back to his radio for some French female luncheon company, boiling eggs to smear with Thousand Island dressing, and waited for his next visitor.

A lost hiker showed up to use his phone; then Rupert to relieve him of accumulated garbage Melba must have told him of, and gossip about

Karl's health. Since the families weren't friendly, Press gave nothing away, especially because auctioneers trolled for properties to empty after a death. No, Karl was all right. Rupert, amused by the drug haul seized at Press's place, observed, "Somebody's in a hole for it. Keep your chin up," he advised, patting Press on the shoulder. "Melba's a good old bird." Rupert laughed. "I was glad to take her in. What a mess. You probably haven't made a hash of your life, so you think you can sympathize with somebody like her that has. But I'm not so sure."

Press, remembering Cos Cob's chapter of AA, invaluable to acquaintances whom he and other straight-laced fellows could not have helped, saw what he meant if Rupert was indeed a benevolent force. Motives were a crisscross, his and Carol's too. At the Clarks' church people were forgiven for their adultery or shoplifting if they repented. Rupert seemed as considerate as Karl regarding Press's handicap yet less at ease, probably because Karl had officiated at so many catastrophes. Rupert wanted to be of service and then gone, but his son Al, "The Hippies' Horse," was less inhibited and formal. Rog, on the other hand, had a more brutal cast, on the watch for wounds that could be exploited.

"I don't know whether I should forgive people or kick myself for suspecting them," Press confided unexpectedly.

"Well, why not both?" Rupert laughed. "Some-body did wrong, but you'll never know who, so fuck it."

Press called Dorothy and then his children after Rupert left. He wanted Carol back, however, teasing him. Instead, a farmer turned up who'd been foreclosed on. The church had sent him so Press could read the papers. Of course Press couldn't, so listened to the farmer read them. Then they got in his car to ride to the bank. The manager—the woman who Karl distrusted because she *was* a woman—patiently explained what they meant, and Press couldn't dispute what she said. "Sorry to be useless," he told the poor man. Asked to be dropped at the Clarks' farm, it being almost milking time.

The milking machines sounded tranquilizing, and there was the collegiality of seventy animal spirits thriving, warming the barn with cud-chewing, nose-snuffling and sisterly mammal-hood. Here every advantage accrued to the farmer whose beasts were content, welcoming the very procedures which earned his income. Two cats rubbed against Press's legs and Avis in passing mentioned the blessings of the Lord.

Carol did come by a day later bestowing a brush-by kiss and inspected the house for other visitations; then led him for a walk-around, his arm pinned round her waist, and after asking, "Are you up for it?" down the stubby trail into the swamp. They scarcely talked, yet he had never been so far or zigzagged so very much before, until she stopped and spun him around, shifting her own position too, so he had no idea where he was.

"Scary," he blurted, both pleased and apprehensive.

"So who's your friend?"

"You are, if you take me back, not play Hansel and Gretel."

"Did Gretel make love with Hansel? Let's see."

She moved close to hug and lead him. He didn't know where, until at last he recognized the arching crowns of his shade trees. "Safe and sound," she gloated. "So now you can discard me."

She led him inside for their old ritual of a hot bath, whereby he was permitted to sit alongside and soap her back. "What footing *are* we on? I missed running into you when you came by the other day," she joked as he dried her. "But you're going to make the fish run to Maine, I hear. That'll be fun."

There were banalities he missed though, like his dentist in Greenwich, who chatted for half of your hour in the chair but was precise enough during the other half. An "angry tooth," he would have called the loose one Press was probing. "It's lost its moorings."

White-collar guy in a blue-collar pickle. No

dentist or doctor, but he did have a Rotary Club to go to if someone would pick him up. He'd been once and paid his dues, talked to the bank manager and pharmacist, and met a high school teacher who'd offered to bring him to a football game if he called. What he wanted was footing. He might mentor a college-bound kid, who he could also dictate letters to. At the Solid Rock Church none had approached him, but how about a football game? So he did call, and the next thing he knew he was in the stands. Although they didn't become close friends, it was exhilarating cheering for North Country Regional High School when they scored and the faculty around him yelled. The quarterback apparently lacked receivers as good as him so they didn't win, but he also boasted a mean curveball, when he pitched in the spring, Press heard. "No problem about a college there," Pete, his host, said. He brought two other students over to shake hands and a couple of teachers too. Press hoped to be invited for a beer afterward, if teachers permitted themselves that, but they seemed committed to showing up at parents' post-game parties. The hubbub reminded him of a different stratum of society he missed. The country-clubbers of Cos Cob at their best. Lawyers, doctors, bankers, who read books and went to concerts, or might be a Sunday painter, arguing nonconformist politics if no one else was listening.

When Pete drove him home, "Tell 'em they don't need to major in Economics to make money. Tell them what makes them happy should be it," he said, but received no response beyond kindly wishes and good-byes.

Press called Dorothy for news of Karl, still tethered to an oxygen tank and making his children's phone calls no picnic for them. When Press himself tried, he muttered quietly that he should have shot himself while he had had the chance. "I could've tripped on a footlog or something. No proof of suicide." He cursed the bank in advance, if they took the house away from Dorothy, already having cashed in his life insurance to pay their bills.

When he went over, Dorothy gave him a chicken sandwich in lieu of lunch, which he apologetically wolfed down before clearing out so she could receive a train of visitors—her many friends.

The swamp was a bedlam of crow caws and owl hoots because of a major dispute, and simmering scents. Sheila, the setter, had accompanied him, wagging, swaying against his legs, but soon returned to her mistress's house.

At his own, the swamp indeed wasn't slumbering. Crows versus hawks or owls continued clamoring, as if at war. An out-of-sync tree frog piped once or twice, and a larger one, presumably green, snored an untimely croak, while the wind flapped like a heron's wings. A loud bird—perhaps an osprey swirling—protested an intrusion. Karl had honed Press's ability to listen. He smelled the usual skunk, heard his chipmunks, and talked to his son, hockey the topic, likely to become Jeremy's favorite sport, though months away. The rink was opening, so kids could practice, and on defense he could skate backward faster than forward.

"God's will," Dorothy invoked, as Karl hung on in a manner he would have preferred to shortcut. She sat by his bed scribbling notes for a column she'd call "A Veteran's Memories," to cut the tension. None of these he would have talked about under ordinary circumstances, lest they sound like "chest-thumping." But now he'd never see anybody who'd read the newspaper so he let her recount the dud German artillery shell rolling into his foxhole at Anzio, then fighting through the mountains nearly clear to Rome. After that, his unit had landed in the south of France, battling north to the hellish burning tanks at the Colmar Pocket. Outside the room she read a draft aloud to Press for suggestions until some of their grown children materialized, each a pincushion of idiosyncrasies, Karl not having been the easiest of pops.

Melba in her still-unregistered car clanked to his door in search of grocery money till her social security check arrived. And did he know about antiques? Rog had stumbled on a clutch of such at a dead widow's house, probably originally from Connecticut, he thought: "Like you, and like the dealer he'll likely sell them to. But he don't want to be taken for a fool."

"He's forgotten I'm blind!" Press laughed. "And we didn't do antiques."

"Rog doesn't forget anything, but he'd like you to feel them or stroke them. He thinks you're classier than him."

They agreed that was funny, though not the deal that Rog would try to foist upon the relatives who wanted to empty the house for sale. Probably would tell them he'd truck the old stuff away for free—not charge them, unless they had plans for it, which, addled as they were, they wouldn't. "Also he wants to know if Karl is dead."

Press sputtered angrily, "No!"

"Rupert was never crooked, you can say that for him. Not as smart a businessman but not a crook. If he'd chiseled you a little, he'd make it up later—like now," she said, meaning lending her the trailer to live out her last days in. She reminisced about when his boys were close, before they went their separate ways. They'd bent some people so out of shape that when a ski-mask bank robbery occurred, the cops suspected them, but couldn't find where the money was to prove it. The miscreants had calmly directed traffic with their deer rifles before the getaway car whisked them away. No big spending or bragging in the saloon, yet the rumor was so persistent that Rupert floated the whisper that his boys had hidden their loot in a cowshit pile. Sure enough, the FBI or troopers had hired a backhoe to dig all through the manure, looking in vain.

Press, spellbound, waited. "So?"

"Oh, nobody got arrested."

*"So?"* he persisted.

"You mean did Al and Rog do it? Well, since there's no proof and it was twenty years ago and since they came to their senses and we're friends, you bet, I think, though no one's told me so."

Press kicked her in the ankle when she didn't go on, and she laughed.

"You want a kicking contest? You don't think I could take advantage and win?"

"You win," he conceded.

"You want to know what they did with the money? Where is it? If it's buried, why wouldn't they dig it up after the heat was off? The word I heard was—and don't say so—they put their bag of money in a freight car and then lost the freight car."

Afraid to kick her again, Press just waited.

"They were smart enough to figure that if they got the wad across the border, nobody would be looking as hard for it in Canada. Our cops don't go there. And the rail line from Montreal to Portland runs through here. So it's like with the

164

drugs. You put a bundle into a boxcar—used to be passenger trains, too—and open it on a siding on the other side. Then it's yours, whichever direction you smuggled it from. So," she continued, after he waited a minute, "Rog and Juliette—she's French anyway, you know—went through the border controls on the highway like normal, to visit her relatives. But when they looked for the car that he and Al had stuck the money in they couldn't find it. Maybe the engineer went right on through to Montreal without stopping anywhere, or they forgot the numbers on the car, or the railroad cops started asking what they were snooping around every railway spur in southern Quebec for. So God knows where the bundle ended up and who spent it."

"They flubbed it," Press agreed.

"They learned their lesson," she concluded, as Rog's car pulled in.

Rog was dismissive of Melba and patronizing toward Press, as he realized the extent of his handicap. He led him out with a bit of a swagger and into his auction house downtown. But Juliette, the Canadian wife, Frenchily perfumed, who handled their larger-scale finances, promptly put an end to that, seating him on a couch with tea. She wanted to read him the list of stocks, like GE and IBM, the "hicktown adviser" had picked for them.

"Good blue chips. Don't try to beat the market and trade." Yet, beyond that, she wanted to ask if he had been to the Metropolitan Museum of Art or the Museum of Modern Art. Rog had never taken her to New York, not to mention Paris—had he been to the Louvre?—where she also deserved to go, considering the money their business had amassed. Renoirs, Picassos she'd seen in Montreal.

Rog interrupted her cultural pining by bringing over a side table for Press to feel—the lines, inlays, and finish. "Should we clean it, oil it? Or would that ruin the patina?"

He showed Press other items he couldn't see and was advised to let the dealer he sold them to make that decision, which of course begged the question of whether the pieces had intrinsic worth. "You know cows, they know breakfronts and bureaus. Take her to Paris," Press laughed, and got a hand-squeeze.

Rog, displeased, asked snidely whether Darryl and Avis might not be glad that Karl was sick, remembering the families' feud after Karl's son had mistreated the Clarks' daughter.

"That's absurd," Press said, but wishing to mollify him, praised the good-guy kindness of his brother Al, not to mention how he enjoyed sitting in the bleachers at his auctions. He dredged up, too, the name of a fancy antique shop in Greenwich whose owner wouldn't stoop to sleaze-ball appraisals even of a hodgepodge of rickety items in a truck with Vermont license plates.

"Sir, I'm glad we've done this," Rog conceded, over the bleating of two lambs in a pen in the background, after Press had fingered a kitchen hutch, a Queen Anne-style chair, a Shaker sort of rocker, and other booty.

Back on Ten Mile Road again, he creaked in his swing on the porch as Melba found excuses to earn some "steak money." Her social security check just paid for macaroni. "Bats! Bats in the belfry?—you don't care, right?"

He wondered whose mental state she was referring to, till she explained that she had discovered actual bats in a corner of the attic where a broken window offered them access.

"Let them live."

"I like horses. You like bats."

"Yes, but I want to hear about those racetracks, when you were sleeping in the straw in the stalls."

"We didn't want some rat slipping our horse a mickey."

"And the rats talk too?"

"Oh sure. The real rats, they talk more than the people do. But they'll defend their turf, so the ones eating your horse's oats won't let a bunch of others in to meddle with you once they know you and you know them."

"And at a rodeo?"

"At the rodeos, you don't sleep under the hooves of a bull or bronco! No, your horse that you ride for roping, she wants to spend all night outdoors in a pasture eating grass. It'd be mean to stick her in a stall."

"I want a parrot," Press suggested frivolously. But Melba had inherited a cockatoo in a house she and one of her husbands had rented.

"*He* didn't like cages; he'd been in jail, so we let it roam the place, fed it good, and didn't clip its wings. And one day the door was open for a moment too long and it flies up into a tree, talking to the jays that hung around, the way it had been doing anyway when it was in the house. Their colors were different but their voices weren't. Anyhow, in a tree, up high. Hadn't been that high maybe ever. The whiskey jacks surrounded it, amazed that it was free. They'd used to yell through the window—'Let my people go!' Yet it didn't really speak their language or know how to fly right. It was bigger, with plumage not built for warmth. So they left—those jays that had hollered through the window like comrades when it was perched inside. There she was, at the top of the tallest tree. Wouldn't come down at sunset when the wind blew cold. At dawn, still freezing there, wouldn't come down for something to eat, or know where to drink. Broke your heart. Died there at the top the next day, rather than surrender and fly down. Just dropped. Braver than you can imagine."

Press waved to Melba's car as she rattled off, having scotched his idea of a bird to talk to.

Then Dorothy turned in, inviting him to the hospital. Karl was free-associating and held his hand. He ruminated about how he'd shot a German soldier from a ridgeline who was indulging in a crap. Also on the subject of war brides. He could have brought one back, taught her English, and installed her on the farm. "Black, black hair." Karl laughed. At the Legion he'd observed a ton of war brides. The Koreans fitted in, so tickled to get clear of Korea, but the English ones sometimes cried at the bleakness of this north country.

Karl dropped asleep just as Benny Messer showed up, so Benny drove Press back to his place, cleared the "skin magazines" off the Mercedes' backseat that served as a divan, and showed him the telescope that he used to spy on the hippies in the meadow up the hill. "I've seen you there!" He wouldn't divulge whether he'd ever had kids or wives or seen the inside of a jail, but good-humoredly suggested half the people Press was hanging out with could have. Benny thought that all the world's a junkyard, so why not live in the midst of it—boilers from starter houses, fridges from failed marriages that garter snakes lived under, he said. A honeymoon dining set discarded the year a doctor found the lump. Stoves on legs, toilets intact. Press smelled motor oil from the totaled cars the cops or wreckers had hauled in. "People forget stuff. Just in the glove compartment, for example, or taped under the spare tire. You find cash. I go through my wrecks; a gold chain, earring, or just a book that's fun to read on the floor in the back."

"You're like an undertaker."

"No, more interesting than that. I see their mistakes, not just the corpse. Like a head-shrinker. If you could see all the junkers in my yard."

"It's a rough world," Press agreed, arm wrestling for a futile second with him. Benny said he'd lay for anybody bothering Press and "twist their ears on backwards." He put a pistol in its holster in his hands.

Delivering Press to his home, Benny spotted Carol and her kids waiting for him, and snickered, "You got a good thing going."

"Hot baths. You should gimme a key," Carol said when he climbed to the porch. The children's voices he was so fond of whooped through the house, using both bathrooms, upstairs and down. Her roof leaked, but because she wasn't sleeping with the guy who had built it for her anymore, he wouldn't fix it. So what should she do?

"A quickie?" he suggested, wondering too if this problem could have instigated her visit: was she fishing for money to hire someone? More seriously, however, a kid or boy of twenty or so was straddling the rooftree of the main house and wouldn't come down. Singing, hooting, crying, he was having a nervous breakdown, she thought, but because of their aversion to established authority the others at the commune weren't calling the cops or for an ambulance. Let him express himself, do his thing, et cetera. He'll wear down, he'll sleep it off.

"Is he high?" A fire truck could handle this but Press knew hippies who swallowed LSD might behave like that, and people wouldn't call for help for fear of drugs around and other legal implications for themselves.

"No, no, no." She explained how he was somebody's troubled kid brother and so had not been kicked out for previous oddities, and was on medication. But certain individuals liked the pills he'd been prescribed—another reason not to have told him to hit the road—so he wasn't actually even getting all of those. "What should I do?"

They sat indoors, a site for grave discussion, while the kids bathed, played, explored, and swung on the tire hanging from the maple tree outside. No, no, she insisted, she hadn't driven to his house so he'd get in trouble with the commune for making the call. "What should we do? The cops know that we eat our placentas or all that crazy stuff on the rumor mill. So either they'll take this kind of thing too seriously, or not at all."

Press disagreed. A policeman as competent as

Karl would home in on exactly what to do. Carol dithered—if only the kid would leave, he'd be his parents' responsibility.

"What would your father do?" Press challenged her, which threw her for a loop. She asked him to go back with her and try to talk the poor boy down.

"Your father could. I'm blind."

"Should we call?"

"Is he threatening to throw himself off?"

"No, he's cantering, he's in heaven, enjoying himself."

They broke out the ice cream for the kids and ate too much themselves. Yet the image of a boy flipping out on a ridgepole could not be ignored. Nor did a phone call to Ten Mile Farm for the latest bulletin relieve their anxiety. They drove, and found that he was off the roof—reportedly asleep in his pup tent or tepee or treehouse. So Carol brought Press to her cabin, fed everybody spaghetti, and let him into her bed with all his clothes on, but put a nipple in his mouth because "You're so good." She told him about a trust-fund freak in another town who'd built a heated swimming pool that any girl could use if she wore no suit. Of course one reason the cops so seldom hassled the hippies was that so many of them had rich pops who could sue the cops.

She couldn't fall asleep easily, however, after watching the boy straddling the rooftop, talking in tongues. "That would be murder," Press obsessed, "if he killed himself because your people stole his medicines for themselves."

Carol stiffened in surprise but not anger. "We're not a monolith." They did go to sleep, loosely clasping each other, and in the morning she got the kids to the school bus and Press to his house.

Hours later, he was cozily ensconced in great Mozart and Bach performances on the radio when startled by a pounding on his door. It was Carol in tears.

"He hanged himself! Overnight! From his tree-house! While we were sleeping." The sheriff was there; his parents flying from Cleveland; his brother—the regular commune member—vomiting, first food, now blood.

Press had once participated in a brokerage meeting on Sixth Avenue where a Merrill Lynch man at the long table had suddenly collapsed next to him and died on the floor. They caught his hands to settle him, to no avail.

Press phoned his wife, as he vividly recalled, hugging Carol. "I'm so sorry. But you didn't do it."

She lay on the couch, breathing heavily though waving her finger to prevent him from turning the music off. He pictured what she was picturing. No, she elaborated, she hadn't seen the body hanging, only his poor body brought to the farmhouse after-ward, where the medical examiner took testimony.

"So much craziness! I'm sick of it," she pronounced, which he understood to mean in such anarchy how could you distinguish real distress? Press refrained from any obvious finger-wagging about the pilfered pills, but did gently murmur that her father's as well as Dorothy Day's Christianity drew "precious boundaries" that sectarian communes didn't have.

"Yes, people OD at these places and not at Dorothy Day's. But this wasn't OD'ing, and I do remember somebody knocking himself off even at the Maryhouse, our Catholic Worker place."

"It wasn't OD'ing," he agreed. Yet weirdos turned up off the road so often at the commune—having heard about it—that you couldn't nurture all of them, especially with no creed in common. He was glad he knew so few up on that hill, and comforted her by touch and hug. She stayed till school let out, then returned so that the family could spend the night with him. The kids however had not been shielded from the news; had heard about the hanging from other commune children at school, and were asking how it was possible to kill yourself that way, and why.

Press treated everybody to a feast at a lakeside restaurant twenty miles away he hadn't been to since Claire and Jeremy and Molly were here.

Wine or Shirley Temples, with lobsters trucked by Carol's Arkansas friend from Maine. He played devil's advocate for a while, suggesting that collateral damage was inevitable in a social experiment like Ten Mile Farm, and a vulnerable soul such as the boy who had hitchhiked to join his brother there might have done the same thing elsewhere. Carol interrupted abruptly in distress because this was a well-heeled family and she recognized the surviving son sitting at another table with, no doubt, his distraught parents. He had an overnight bag beside his chair, she said, as if he might be leaving Ten Mile Farm for good.

That might be for the best, but my god the grief. "And he's looking at us!" she whispered. "Eatin' a lobster, boiled alive."

A jumbo guilt trip. After the school week, the three of them would drive downcountry to Granddad's, the kids were delighted to hear. But the choices Carol could discuss, she observed to Press sotto voce, were limited ones. She had picked a father for her children who lived on the Hudson with another woman and preferred she stay off in Vermont. And she had copied her father's livelihood of stained-glass art, but if you weren't a well-known church-window craftsman and devout like him, there was no living in it. All food stamps, instead, and Aid to Families with Dependent Children—the latter requiring you to name the father, if you were a single mom, which she was unwilling to do. A sympathetic female bureaucrat had put down "Unknown" on the form for her.

"List me," Press joked, although that would only lead to being sued.

The dead boy's family left for whatever hotel would contain their grief for tonight, which lightened the atmosphere enough for Press, as the non-driver, to grow tipsy. The kids were toying with extra desserts and Carol felt too buried in reflection to hurry them up.

# Chapter 8

Karl succumbed at home without Press realizing he had returned there. At his own request of course, and the house was filled with the town's solid citizenry when the Clarks informed Press what had happened. Legionnaires, fire chiefs from hither and yon, women bearing casseroles and fresh baked breads. He felt welcome but superfluous and kissed Dorothy and left.

Blindness he had noticed brought you back to basics, so he sorted through his larder for last-ditch foods. Raisins, bananas, cans that you could open without cooking the contents, because he didn't trust himself around the stove anymore. Isolated, vulnerable, he wanted to pay for Melba's car to be repaired and registered immediately and maybe to install a phone for her. He handled innumerable cans but needed somebody to separate the peaches from the corn, the pears, the peas.

The Clarks had heard also about the commune suicide. EMTs and deputies had trundled up the hill to witness the naked boy displayed in all his frailty. Having jumped from the tree limb with a noose around his neck, his hands, as one guy told Darryl, still gripped the rope, as though he might have changed his mind but not been strong enough to pull himself back up.

The Clarks wanted their Solid Rock Gospel Church to hold a service of some sort for the dead hippie, since Press confirmed that after the body was surrendered by the police to his parents, probably no religious memorial would occur on the hill. "They have a bunch of spiritualities, from Buddhist to Hindu," he explained. "But they would just have buried him there."

"A hodgepodge," Avis said. But the minister wouldn't consent because no one, including Press, had even known the erring soul. And Karl's death in the meantime distracted everybody. In their living room, Press knelt with the Clarks to pray for the boy and other searchers up the hill. They pumped Press for further information about "the cult," as they dubbed the commune, but he called it a counterculture instead and doubted Karl's white-collar son was the one who had dumped their daughter at the altar, a continuing peeve but no one mentioned that. It was a time for forgiveness.

While Carol was gone, the Arkansas man— actually from San Diego he said—knocked on the door to propose Press take the ride to Portland with him. And Press liked the idea. He seemed more worldly than the other "freaks," had been to New Orleans, Seattle, and Mexico, and didn't hit Press up for any money. In fact he'd been to

Germany in the military and so was more informed, less knee-jerk anti-war than other hippies. He gave his name as Chuck and said he'd been at Ten Mile's sister commune in Arkansas for the pussy, but left in order not to step on anybody's toes. "You know how that is." They sat in Press's Adirondack chairs on the lawn so that, inside, he couldn't case the joint, so to speak. His acquaintance with Carol did not predate arriving here and yet already he patched her roof's leak, he said; he'd come because a pal of his had had this fish-run gig before. Pipe fitting was his trade. Wanted to go to Saudi Arabia but in Maine he should find work.

Press wondered what he looked like. Rawboned and burly, wiry? And when he smiled, was it a smirk or grin, frank or sly? Press decided to wait and talk to Carol before embarking on a trip.

At Karl's funeral there were testimonials recounting barn fires and Karl's saving the church steeple. With his hands clasped by numerous unknown individuals, he realized his condition enabled him to cross social barriers like summer person versus year-rounder, hippie versus Bible-believer, white-collar and hardscrabble. Dorothy wasn't the only woman who kissed him, for example, and somebody offered him board and lodging for a modest stipend. The state, indeed, paid private families to house indigent oldsters and autistic adults.

Carol had returned so the children wouldn't miss school, but wasn't cheery. Her father had stabilized her mood about solving any problems. That is, you can't save everyone who wants to die, and art is not for making money. Uncle Sam was feeding her, a single mother, so for the year ahead she could explore her talent for jigsawing glass—he'd provided boxes of it. She shouldn't kick herself because the commune was dysfunctional. Be upright in your own life. Did every church he worked in uphold the Golden Rule? Greedy people gazed at his windows from the pews. The sexual license prevalent among Carol's sixties generation was deplorable, but no more than predatory Capitalism, with cruel slums alongside absurd affluence: affluence which paid for his depictions of the Holy Family as a form of expiation. Love was the basis for what he believed. Promiscuity certainly violated that polestar, yet caring for others, even in "fooling around"—which was not to justify it—topped dog-eat-dog Capitalism.

"He sounds centered. Terrific," Press told her. "I'd like to meet him. He must love the children, you've done so well with them."

"You bet."

Not lovey-dovey, she vanished for a few days to realign herself at Ten Mile Farm, where people might have been ignored as part of freedom's ideology. When the rubber hit the road, freedom had its complications.

Press lay low for a while too, letting Dorothy's bereavement proceed with her daughter who had flown from California, and her high school friends for company. After arguing aloud with the chat show personalities, he stuck with the French bands on the radio. His dependence on the Clarks for shopping errands was a balancing act. Too much would strain their patience. They believed in tithing energy as well as money, 10 percent in good works—far more than most folks budgeted for kindness—though they couldn't fill in for his daily lunch at Dorothy's.

Hearing about the two deaths, Melba turned up, "like a bad penny," she joked, and fried him an egg and roasted a chicken, besides scrubbing the house. "Still looking for where you hide your money!" But in the meantime she told him she'd gotten the inspection sticker for her car, with his money, partly because the garage guy's father stepped in for her.

"You helped his father lose his cherry too?"

"You think your hippie friends invented giving good head? I used to have a doctor treat me free so he could feel me up."

Without needing to discuss it, their new notion of the frequency and duration of her visits jibed. She bought him fruits and salads, being familiar from hotel work what people like him ordered. Then might tell him, as an aperitif, how when she cleaned rooms at a downscale motel, she used to jump in the swimming pool in her blouse when she got sweaty but continue working with it clinging to her breasts for all to see.

"Great!" he muttered, while munching red and green peppers on a plate of greens.

She identified painfully, though, with the dead boy's parents, her own son having been about the same age when he went missing in the Absaroka mountains, "looking for," as she put it, his father. Not that that reprehensible guy had actually been there, but imitating what he conceived his "mountain man" dad to have been like. "God, I was in a tailspin. A year, two years, like a vacuum."

Press went to Dorothy's occasionally for tea instead of lunch, when she found she missed their routine. She had writer's block, she said, so talking with him in a civilized fashion might break her into fluency, not just the old beaver trappers who were dropping in with their condolences. Press suggested them for a column, the bear-hounds men, fur buyers, and fire-ladder men who'd loved her husband.

Yet all was not peaceful. He heard voices from the trail to the swamp again, and a car maybe meeting them at the head of his drive. "Snitches get stitches and end up in ditches," he recalled from a radio program, and so his dilemma was unchanged from months ago. It even rattled his trust in Melba. Had she been planted to observe him? Next time she showed up, with brie and Camembert and classy crackers, squash soup and French tarts from the market, he was disarmed as she unloaded her bags of goodies.

He did mention the voices, but Melba replied, "A hundred fucking years ago there were scumbags on that path." She paused. "No, I'm not moving in with you. I like my trailer and the horses at the window."

"I didn't ask you to."

"No, you're not that desperate, with those thugs in the swamp." She laughed.

"Rich people are thuggish too, you know. I've dealt with some. Or their trust fund is as holey as a sieve and they'll call you from Bali."

"Bali beats Vegas."

"I had them in Vegas too, till you have to cut them loose and they wail and whine like Mommy died all over again."

"What a downer. I've walked out on a few like that."

He biked over to Dorothy's the next day, who was stewing a bit with all of Karl's clothes laid out to be stored or else disposed of. The radio scanner was off, and there'd been a fistfight at the firehouse. "Karl would turn over in his grave if he knew that." Those men "had your back." And the animals missed him. Even the crows flying over hollered for an answer. Their rapport felt gummed up, however, without Karl's presence as a lubricant. Talking across him in the kitchen had emphasized what they had in common. She treated Press a little like the summer campers she'd sold cottage cheese to in her youth.

He found a note wedged in his door, in block letters yet exasperating because he couldn't read it—called Cos Cob to be sure no family emergency was involved. He laid it on the table and listened to Virgil Fox exulting on the organ, king of instruments, then napped, dreaming of a craggy trail with figures descending toward him.

Knocking woke him. The Arkansas character— "I go by Chuck"—presumed Press had read the note and was fetching him "to the healing ceremony." Amenable as usual, he climbed into the truck and felt the road curve appropriately up toward Ten Mile Farm. Hands led him to the big meadow and seated him in the grass—was *he* to be healed? He smelled barbeque sauce. By and by somebody handed him a hot dog on a fork and a can of beer as families gathered and dusk fell. A circle formed. The cooking fire rose into a bonfire.

He waited for Carol. She did materialize and took his hand, as another woman did on the other side. Beyond Carol, he heard Chuck's voice, but she was distracted. "Things are falling apart. I want to suggest something," she murmured confusedly. A man was rhythmically pronouncing the Zen chant "Om."

Press had figured out that the healing ritual he was now a part of was for the commune as a whole and therefore concerned the poor youngster's suicide. He also knew she disliked speaking publicly, yet did she mean things were falling apart personally or for the group? The nervous pulsing of her hand gripping his asked for moral support. "Rules, we need rules."

"A very bad thing happened three days ago. We have to reckon with it, cleanse ourselves, and mourn," The Dad announced. A silence followed, until a scattering of voices began recalling the boy's month-long stay. Such a mishap was "the cost of freedom," someone said.

But Carol disagreed agitatedly. "No. That's letting us off the hook."

A comment that "the land has been damaged" made Press wince. Clumsily, sincerely, other voices testified to their own "crash landings" on this mountain and how it had saved them. "This is sanity. It's not sane out there. Look what we've accomplished."

Carol chipped in again, "We ought to set up a kind of council, about membership and policies. A sort of legislature." A man across the circle asked how that might have saved the hapless kid. "Freedom is dangerous."

But Carol did have an undertone of less vocal support.

"A gatekeeper," Press offered, adding his two

cents' worth. But he was answered with arguments about the illogic of living off the grid with gatekeepers.

"We shouldn't have kept him," The Dad agreed. "It drew attention."

"But policies. A council for ground rules," Carol persisted.

Certain male voices seemed to suspect where she was going and wanted to head her off. Several women supported her euphemistically, however, by referring to cops being around. The Dad refereed with amusement. "The City Council," he called the idea. "But smoke it, don't sell it? Should we elect our own cops?"

Laughingly he didn't take sides, but the druggies did. They wanted their money. Those lucrative trips to Brooklyn. And no male voices augmented Carol's doubts. A woman blurred the discussion by suggesting that social workers might be brought in. She was known for nursing her little boy in public though he was turning five. The stoners hooted in support of her.

"We accept people, acid and all, no questions asked." Sentiment was swinging against using this off-kilter visitor's death to formalize the valuably disorganized lifestyle at Ten Mile. Creeps could be shouldered out pronto after they arrived. The squalid square world wasn't perfect either. A Council smacked of regimentation, "and we have something precious."

The Dad, like a tillerman, let the winds blow idiosyncratically, till afterward he'd speak to the losers. Just so, he had fathomed Carol's viewpoint. "We were asleep at the switch. Our eyes and ears should have prevented that. And the pot-growing's got to get under cover," he said in passing. "You put yours in the cornfield, where the pig plane can't spot it."

Of course her concern had been that money hustles like drug peddling undermined The Farm, not how to conceal them. "We failed, but you were my moral support," she told Press, serving him cornbread and carrots to complete his picnic supper. The sky seemed anciently velvet, the breeze sweet with leafy perfume, and people remained roundabout in what was indeed a healing process.

Chuck, in Carol's hearing, asked Press if he would go over some paper with him. "I don't read good."

"Neither do I." They laughed. "Have you got kids in Arkansas or San Diego?"

"I won't tell you where I have kids. But it's not child support. It's loan papers. I'm buying a car," he chuckled, and drove Press home.

Payment schedules was the topic of the day, plus trade-in details. Fine print was read to him by the dealer and Chuck, who appeared to be dyslexic, queried the terms with Press's help. Apparently he had no credit history except for an Exxon card and had brought two thousand cash for a down payment because he didn't believe in banks. The dealer wouldn't have gone through with it for a new car, but this one just had eighty thousand fewer miles on it than the truck he was turning in, and when he was asked for another thousand dollars in earnest money up front, Chuck came up with it.

"I can see why you brought a blind man. He can't rob you."

Chuck, triumphant behind new wheels after "signing on the dotted line," said driving was as good as sex for him; he loved it. He suggested driving into Canada "for Frog food," for the restaurants on his list, with the temporary plates, but settled for just two pepper steaks in town because the paper trail wouldn't have cleared.

"Sure I've got kids. They'll look me up when they want a trade. Their stepdad's a loser, the salesman type. Nothing solid in that. I can go to Alaska or anywhere. Sign for a year, and free airfare. So you pick a hotel you want to winter in in Florida or on the Gulf when the snow flies, and in fact, I'll drive you down, cheap as a plane."

When Press asked why these communes, "No lease. Free love," Chuck explained, and they laughed. But he loved the Kaw River—Kansas River—"Special. I'll go back." His old lady in California had wanted him to put his money in a car wash or pair with her brother as a house painter, so he wouldn't travel. "Look for me among the hippies," he advised any private dick that might be trailing him. His boys would find him when they wanted to.

That image, alas, brought Melba's lost sons to mind. Maybe desperados like her and this chump weren't bored by him because they felt a link to that flip of a coin which determined that one man had it all and the next was blind.

"Yep. A fork in the road," Press teased—Saudi Arabia or fish—remembering the pistol in the glove compartment of the truck being transferred to the Chevy.

On the drive home, Press regretted allowing himself so little freedom of the road when he'd been young. The straight and narrow had claimed him. And even now, car jaunts with Jeremy and Molly were beyond him.

They gossiped about The Dad, a mystery man who had had a garage band in New Jersey and half-graduated from music school before becoming a "group therapist" here. The Ozark commune was started by a classmate of his from Little Rock.

"How about Carol?" Press asked.

"Another good soul. But I'm to tell you about Carol?"

"Well, what I don't know."

"Pussy is pussy. The long-assed type, though I like compact. But if you're getting some don't ask questions."

"I envy you being able to jump in your car."

In his kitchen, Press thumped his head against the wall in frustration.

One hippie he knew, by contrast, had ridden a stallion to San Francisco and back. Another had bicycled across, also a stunt befitting a different stage of life but unmatched in his memories. He was getting his ticket punched, fortifying his resume. Others traveled the famous counter-conventional trail from Istanbul to New Delhi by bus or thumb through Iran and Afghanistan. And afterward, enlarged by the experience, they went into the export-import business or a multi-national corporation.

To stabilize himself, and after calling Connecticut and finding his children not at home, he walked to Dorothy's for a bit of solace. She was nostalgi-cally regretful. "I saw an hourglass in the clouds." Karl had never gone with her to New York so she could see a play or go to the great museums. Like other veterans of the war, combat had shown him all the Europe he wanted exposure to. Press remembered Rog's wife Juliette also complaining about never having gotten to the Big Apple, and invited Dorothy to go with him.

Speculating with a smile in her voice, Dorothy answered that she'd hate to look like a hick. "Except if I was guiding you around these places you already know it would lend me a veneer."

"*I* could be the redneck from Peoria, yet whisper

to you so you'd ask for the Rembrandts and Monets." Press found himself imagining climbing the classic steps of the Met with his arm linked in hers, and the joy of resonance in those sculpture galleries and exhibit halls. He still had maintained his membership in the Harvard Club, as if for a last hurrah, so could reserve separate rooms and do it right.

Ruefully she suggested, "I'll never leave here." In her teens she'd ridden her brothers' Christmas tree truck to sell bales of firs on Twenty-Third Street in Manhattan—a doorman letting them use the service lavatory—"but never went back. Not meant to be. We each have a row to hoe."

"You sound like Avis. 'Jesus was my travel agent.'"

"Yes," she agreed, unswayed but amused. Yet he sensed there might be an opening for a trip south. The Holmewood Inn would delight her, and then the short drive to Central Park, not to mention the Club off Fifth Avenue.

"I owe you lots of hospitality."

"My family's been selling summer people hospitality as long as Karl's was selling rotgut to the Woodchucks," Woodchucks being Vermonters of the type who hibernated in the winter or moseyed about drinking moonshine otherwise. Widowhood, "At Sixes and Sevens," was her current column topic and its "danger of running off the rails," so he told her she was doing a pretty good job.

"The school's dismal, the neighbors freaky. No role models," Carol railed on his porch the next day. She was sick of counting food stamps and disheartened at selling zero artwork for the past three months. Chuck had started hitting on her too, after the roof leak.

"On the other hand, growing up beside a brook that you can drink out of seems like a pretty promising beginning to me. Abraham Lincoln had it just about the same. We ought to try going on a sales trip with your collages, don't you think? They're so beautiful." She had hung glasswork in his windows where the sun hit.

He stroked her, rediscovering her lanky height and straight long hair. She remained too antsy to come inside the house, yet wanted comforting and squeezed his hand. Really, he emphasized, children create their own advantages, and the high school had good teachers whom he'd met at the football game, while his own fancy prep school—when you went to reunions—had turned out some incredibly dull specimens. "We could rent a car to show your work," Press proposed.

"I have a good dad, but I do need a fairy goddad. The trick is, when you've been trained to do church art—then, if you no longer believe in what the windows are about, how do you operate?"

She liked to mix and blend, brindle with verdigris, a starfish near an angel's wings, Quaker

192

silence, Buddhist silence, a touch of the Jain. Still, why not try glassblowing, or paint on slate?

"Sounds goopy," she said, "no traction," though she granted that she should have gone to art school, not just apprenticed with her father. But since his work was celebrative at heart and hers rooted in that same vein too, Christian communitarianism could segue into anarchist communes such as Ten Mile Farm.

"We could take your kids to Quebec City, almost like a trip to Europe, wouldn't that be fun?" he suggested. She'd never been to Europe herself, he realized, with nine children in her family— round-numbered Catholicism.

"You're sweet," she answered unenthusiastically, yet still awaited input from Press. Maturity. Wisdom.

Melba appeared at this juncture, lightening the quandary. "It's only the scrubwoman! You'll have your harem with you, after I mow the lawn."

"Oh yeah, my odalisques. We were talking about a trip to the big city—look at Renoirs—if you want to join us."

"I've seen my share of nudes, but thank you anyway," she replied, and, assuming Press meant New York, "You'll stay at the Waldorf. I don't pay nothing. I sleep in the straw at the Garden, with the horses. Madison Square Garden," she added, since they didn't know what she was talking about. "I won the Barrel Race, in my time."

Press, laughing, explained to Carol that the rodeo world was being invoked, and to Melba that such a jaunt was "above our pay grade."

Melba, though, kept talking about the New York waterfront, a few blocks west of the Garden, where she'd walked between performances and wanted to stow away on one of those great passenger ships named after a queen.

"Oh boy, I envy you." He offered Melba a ginger ale, and she offered to cook lunch for both of them.

Carol groaned, yet Press sensed it was internal, not a rejection. "Settle down. Men dumped me right and left," Melba told her. "Left me on the curb. We were changing cities and I was standing with my suitcase. But off he goes, by his self. Oh, was I lonesome."

"Couldn't have said it better. Join the club," Press chimed in, although he knew Carol's blues did not relate to a single episode like him and Claire.

She sighed, wanting to leave, wanting to stay. "No, I'm always on a tangent."

Melba was disarmed. "I've got chops for you."

"Nice of you, but I'm going to lie down," Carol murmured.

"Been there. And they hump us like a dog on your leg." Both of them laughed, the gentler sex, and Press felt oddly as though Melba and Carol were two ends of a balancing pole, particularly when Melba added that women were "lifesavers" and Carol's lips clicked in a smile.

His own face might have called for elaboration because Melba conceded, "We're rattlebrained, agreed. And if you give us your boys to raise, we'll make them the same as we complain about. Rifles at twelve, and so on. So what do we do about this buckaroo? Don't want to play nursemaid, but he's marooned himself on this desert island where the bears hoot and the herons eat baby alligators down south all winter to get fat for flying up here in the spring."

"Scary. A crash landing." Carol laughed. "Except he can always buy his way out, whereas I can't even pay for a therapist."

They left him to his thoughts, which bobbed like a raft in a calmer sea. Winds from Labrador and Alabama alternated overhead, with miles of tree scent lending pungency. Day by day, was Melba's mantra, like Carol's memory of Dorothy Day.

In New York, while living in a Catholic Worker dormitory, besides kitchen work and mopping, Carol had been assigned to hospice stints at nearby hospitals, holding hands with dying patients who lacked relatives around. Carol did carom back after a couple of days. "I'm flailing." He wished he could see her face. "At Dorothy Day's you could recharge maybe and we'd go to Bleecker Street and hear a sax."

"Let me take you shopping for something nice."

She drew a breath and paced the porch. "That's so sweet a thought, thank you. So generous," she repeated, as if distancing herself without saying no. "It's more than nice, in fact. *I should shop,* it's been so long."

In her car, joshing with each other, spurred by the moment, they made a circuit of several thrift shops and rummage-sale locations where she ordinarily acquired her clothes. Though he pointed out he had meant going to New York, she gushed, "It's a godsend now when the summer people leave and don't want to pack their stuff." The pickings were ripe, often scarcely worn. "I can't believe it. So much. I could wear different things for a week! But I don't feel like a road trip. If you want one, that loose cannon Chuck can run you to Portland and back."

# Chapter 9

Dorothy's friends rallied around, perhaps more comfortable in the house now that Karl wasn't present to remind them that their husbands were shirking fire department service or hadn't been in the military. Press wasn't odd man out at the kaffeeklatsches, but felt more like an object of charity than before, with conversations around him he couldn't join but extra sandwiches pushed on him to carry home. His hope of remaining a part-time boarder, or shifting to full-time soon, was eluding him. He was a sort of Good Samaritan project, as Dorothy bloomed in her womanly circles, sympathetic, perceptive, over tea and cards, and Karl not there to bring up the Legion's Auxiliary duties for them to cook or plan for. Spiky and demanding, he was missed, but Dorothy, independent now, simply suggested, "Bring 'em up!" when Press raised the subject of a visit south for her to meet his kids and possibly continue on to Broadway and even the two Mets, for opera or art. She was flourishing as is.

He missed lying in bed spoon-style with his wife, one hand on the cello shape of her sweet body; Carol didn't sleep with him. In fact, she seemed more distant, worrying about her children's future here "in the bush" once again.

She'd begun phoning that guy on the Hudson—that so-called "poet"—who by her choice had inseminated her for both of her kids.

The trouble was, some woman always answered. Did he have a new partner? She couldn't ask.

Melba was no problem, though. He bought her a hundred-pound sack of oats to feed through the window to her horses, and this pleased her immensely. He felt a bit dumb for not having thought of it before.

Chuck—who'd traded in his Arkansas pickup for the car with temporary plates—swung by "on Carol's say-so" for the fish run to Portland, if Press wanted to go. "You only live once."

True. Press tucked necessities into an overnight bag and climbed in, cane and all, not omitting his passport. "Gone fishing" was what they said here. The smell was of sandwiches and coffee, but he sniffed for clues of who the car had belonged to before. A lady, a plasterer? Chuck drove east toward New Hampshire with careless aplomb, like a man who might put fifty thousand miles on a car's odometer every year or two. Blindness curtained much of the beauty they were passing but not his sense that it was there. White spots checkered his vision. How did people manage blind from youth?

Chuck complained that his parents had sent his less talented brother to college, but not him. But after all what did it matter and he dropped out.

"Nine to five," Chuck laughed, dismissing him, whereas *he'd* shipped out of Long Beach for the Philippines, Bombay, Mombasa. "And yet the girls are ashore," he explained. "But wow, I was weirded out at The Farm. This girl there likes to drink your cum right out of the condom when it's over. A vitamin freak."

"Internal combustion," Press responded with amusement, listening to the GM engine.

The miles spun. They arched high until the White Mountains gave way to Maine's softwood forestlands cut by creeks. "It's nice when it's nice," Chuck said of the weather. Spoke of eating javelina steaks in Arizona. And then of being in a house that was practically full of money, but you'd better pretend you hadn't seen it. "Variety is the spice of life," he recited. This gig he'd picked up from another Ten Mile hippie. The big supermarket chains like Shurfine used their own trucks of course, but he delivered to the smaller stores. Flounder, cod, sole, lobsters, bluefish, bass. The wind smelled yeasty, hopping through the wavy trees.

Chuck hummed and talked about the inshore lobstermen versus the cod boats that went way to the Outer Banks for deeper prize money. Dangers there. He confided that he wore a money belt because he dealt with so many individuals, both on the waterfront, then selling their catch to the storekeepers back in Vermont. Press happened to remember a story on the radio about how Vermont's murky border with Canada was not the only conduit for drugs. Fisher folk might run clear out to international waters and intersect with a mothership to ferry the junk in, hidden among a hold full of fish.

Chuck said it was lonely at sea but "umbilical if you know what I mean." He drove nonstop, except for gas, to a modest motel, the Sleepy Eye, on a lake near the coast where they already knew him. In his room Press napped like a log at first, exhausted. Alone when he woke, he tried to summarize what he'd learned about Chuck, a little disturbed after overhearing him on the phone refer to himself as "Garth." Yet he enjoyed his company nevertheless, as in boyhood memories of when he had hitchhiked all over a bit with strangers. The other kids were playing tennis at their country clubs, but he'd wanted his summers not preppy, just as at school he played hockey not squash during the winter. Being fluid not buttoned-down had been useful at Merrill Lynch because a window-washer might walk in with a million-dollar settlement he wanted to invest that he'd gotten when his rigging broke, or a widow suddenly rich but unsophisticated. If he'd climbed the ladder higher his prep school connections might have helped, but he'd stayed in the infantry.

Vegetating in his room, Press wished he could call Carol or Melba. Paying for a line to Carol's would be prohibitive, not to mention her disinclination for interruptions. But Melba might allow him to connect her trailer to the world. "At your beck and call"—he could hear her sarcastic response. He sat eye to eye with a news commentator's face on the television. Then in the lobby, where he snagged snatches of dialogue, partly because he was paying more attention or simply because he may have seemed inert and therefore harmless. When did people develop laughter paleolithically, he wondered? Did chimpanzees do it? He also calculated as best he could an estimate of his assets: bonds, bank, stocks, et cetera. He used to like to take a flyer on a startup, feel courted with the conference calls, golf dates, a chocolate martini, or go in with a hedge fund.

The desk clerk was a chatty, sympathetic single mom whose ex-husband, she said, was living in a homeless shelter in Boston and trying to persuade their daughter to lend him money, since she wouldn't.

"Good for you. Men are beasts," Press suggested so they could laugh together. She offered him a licorice stick and invited his help on a crossword puzzle. Who stayed here he wondered? Honeymooners and pipeline hunks. The lake was said to be beautiful, she told him, by people who hadn't been looking at it all their lives.

When Chuck called to ask her to give Press a

supper sandwich because he'd found some newbie buddies to drink with at a roadhouse, she did, although the Sleepy Eye served no meals beyond the complimentary muffin and coffee at breakfast. A call or two came in for Chuck himself but not from individuals who volunteered their identity. Press, however, was treated considerately by the lady at the desk and her successor. He turned off the TV because the second one preferred a raffish radio host, who, with the gab of customers checking in or seeking solace, provided diversion enough until Press went back to bed.

Chuck reappeared, his arrangements complete for an early departure. At dawn, he put Press in the car, returned to the port, packed crates of fish, presumably, in the trunk, and they hit the road with the sunrise behind them.

Weaving out of Portland and into rural terrain, Chuck chortled happily. "I was telling this guy to get his ass oiled. He's going to jail. Been sentenced. Has a week or two to turn himself in. Scared shitless of getting raped."

Press was at a loss for words. Finally he said, "So it happens? Have you been in jail?"

"You do the crime, you pay your time."

"So you were?"

"No. I put my dukes up. It might happen to a greenhorn, or if you were a real pain in the ass to the guards, they could put you overnight in a cell with a certain muscleman who was a fag and when they let you out in the morning you could hardly walk, your asshole hurt so much."

"So you never went back?" Press asked hesitantly.

"You mean boomeranged, to the lockup? I've had my issues. AA and whatnot. Going out in the snow and lying down to let it snuff me." When Press's hand groped toward the glove compartment, Chuck brushed his hand aside. "You don't mind armaments there. Take the chance to snooze."

The way waltzed slowly around furry hills. Willie Nelson, Johnny Cash, the Carter family, or Loretta Lynn on the radio. The scent of Christmas trees was salted with clean deep-sea whiffs of brine and the "Coal Miner's Daughter" for company. Press napped, rocking to the dips and curves of the road. Chuck was even reminded of one he knew, a coal miner's daughter he'd like to revisit down in Alabama. "And don't tell anybody I may not stick here all winter."

A siren did sound when Chuck grew too nonchalant in mid-Maine. The trooper, however, needed no convincing that fish was their cargo and a reason for haste, and a blind guy's presence—he walked around to the passenger window to check—helped. Chuck averted a ticket. "Got a warning," he crowed. "Luck of the Irish!" He whistled likably, as the White Mountain Range rose in profile on the left.

Press ruminated on the risks of an ambitious marriage like his had been. Tainted motivations bring a reckoning. You marry someone snappier for climbing the network, but fall off yourself. Serves you right?

Chuck was talking about the traveling life. A legal-age girl for instance, working in her parents' laundromat who felt trapped and wanted to clear out, when you stopped for the night, did your laundry, and talked to her, then went to bed in the motel next door. Yet, emerging next morning, going out to your car and unlocking it, then returning to fetch your luggage, you climb in, speed off, whereupon a voice from the floor of the backseat pleads, "It's just me. So don't freak out. Just take me somewhere. I can call them from there, and they won't know who helped me out."

"Must be okay," Press agreed. Transport was the coin of the realm and your slate got clean. But the gossip at the Solid Rock Church lately concerned a boy who was missing in the next town. Had he lit out for the West as his parents hoped, or had something happened to him?

He mentioned this to Chuck. "What do you think?"

Chuck grunted, groaned, "I dunno. I did hear about that. I guess I would bet he was humping some junk and probably messed up."

"I heard there was a guy over there, an Italian,

who comes to his door with a pistol in his hand." Press paused.

"You mean if you knock?" Chuck laughed. "I wonder. Exiled from Jersey? A mob guy? Sure, no, it would be a helluva mistake for a local kid to work for *him*."

"And our hippies don't?"

"No, no. They might hump stuff over the mountain for themselves, but if you come from Brooklyn you sure don't mess around with a Sicilian guy."

Skipping the deliveries, Press was dropped at his lonely house, glad that his thermostat had kept it warm. No Carol to quiz him, but wanting her to quiz him. That didn't happen for nearly a week, as she "got on with her life." Melba showed up for her regular "shift," as she put it, however, slurping a mop around the floor by the sound of it. Not that he cared how clean his place was, but he wanted the chat and the reassurance of a warm meal in the oven for nightfall. Wranglers she'd been good to was her usual topic, or dirty tricks Rog the auctioneer would play. "The Widow's Nemesis," Press suggested, although not believing all the bad stories, any more than all her yarns of buckaroos. She agreed to his idea for a phone.

He even persuaded Melba to take him home with her to Rupert's place; she had a little terrier that ate the rats she trapped, so they stopped for dog kibble. Her trailer seemed cramped for a permanent abode, but boasted a woodstove, a kitchen table, padded lounge chair, and piles of blankets she said Rupert salvaged from the dump. Her bedsprings were supported by stacked cans of food two feet or a yard high. They were a source of pride. If either social security or Rupert cut her off, she could survive. Press fingered a can, and her reading lamp, and the pup she slept with, and the nuzzling noses of the three horses who trotted close when Melba whistled them in.

He stepped outside and felt the musculature and mane of the tamest mare, till her tail switched his face.

"She gotcha! You got too fresh. I wish I would have done that to the horny dudes."

Trying out her La-Z-Boy, he imagined the dimensions of her life. Rainy days. Bright days. When he asked about Rupert, she said the less she laid eyes on him the better, though Press suspected a false bravado there. She was living on Rupert's largesse, after all, and conceded good qualities in him, like impulsiveness yet decisiveness, and those knowledgeable hands when manipulating cattle in an auction ring. And he knew everybody he needed to know; "But not so smart with a bank statement."

As for the phone, "I may need you as much as you need me."

"And vice versa."

"Yep, lay me out in my finery."

"I will, and you'll notify my next of kin."

"Righto. Who are they? I'm writing it down. And who's Tonto if we're gonna be pardners?"

"Well, Tonto probably had longer hair. Did yours hang down to your belly button?"

"It covered my boobs, if you want to know." Her voice sounded young.

"Yum, yum. I always liked that."

"Oh, I'd look like a chimpanzee if you could see me."

"I don't believe you, and I can't."

"In sickness and in health!" Melba intoned, as if mimicking Claire's wedding vow. "Oh, I could wake the dead, pant, pant, pant, like a metronome—those boys' breathing, if you let them touch you. Darryl Clark, Karl Swinnerton, Rupert, and Rog. Or then go home to Mary Five Fingers."

"Were you a ball-breaker?"

"No, I like men. Without men what do we have? The old ones too."

They split a beer, and when the horses had snuffled enough of a snack out of her hands, she drove him home and fluffed an apple walnut salad for him in the cherrywood bowl. "It's the life of Riley," she said, "until your money runs out."

Ninepin thunder, pelting rain, a coon in the garbage can, loose slats rattling somewhere in the wind, and the vulnerability of owning outbuildings

207

he couldn't see: Wasn't this a fool's errand? Maple Lane was the closest assisted-living facility he'd heard about. Shouldn't he just move there, and keep this place for sentimental visits, perhaps, or a legacy his kids might enjoy, and let Carol live here in the meantime? Or he could scurry to Florida and install himself on a beach somewhere. Northern ice was not his métier. Had he hit a wall, though with a handicap, you always wondered whether everything could really be blamed on that, not your lame foolishness? How quickly, for example, without organized exercise your muscles began to wither—yet what a bore abstract exercise became. He walked on the road, enjoyed a ricey meal at the commune, and helped Carol finance three trips to craft fairs, where she sold some window hangings and medallions. She was still calling that guy on the Hudson, but he wouldn't give his new woman the boot. Nor did she, apart from the personal humiliation, want Christie and Tim living in a fucked-up situation. Here such irregularities were tucked away in shacks and tepees a quarter-mile apart.

What happened, however, was that a resident pothead lent his cabin to two druggies from the city who had never used a woodstove before, and their bedspread caught on fire. They were so high at the time they were lucky to escape as the place burned down. For Press, and Carol too, it seemed to embody how haphazard and half-assed the whole operation had become. Not a going concern.

Press began calling call-in shows to register his two cents' worth on current issues or complain about the "ego trips" of certain presenters. His pledge to see Carol's kids through college hadn't registered unduly. "You've got your own," she said. A bird-call project—learning from the tapes a friend had sent—was vanishing as migration proceeded apace. He'd hear sundry flocks swirl over the swamp, collecting adherents. Dorothy still welcomed his drop-ins on his "constitutionals," remarking how the dog Sheila missed a male presence now that Karl was gone. At the Solid Rock he was perpetually accepted, but sensed that after hearing so many of the other parishioners' confessions, there must be an expectation that he ought to get up on his two hind legs and make some show or presentation of his own, being divorced, after all, which was a no-no. And mustn't they tacitly wonder whether he was playing both ends against the middle by hanging out for so long with both their church and Ten Mile Farm?

And, indeed, he did propose to Carol that they go down to the city so she could revisit Dorothy Day at the Catholic Worker on Houston Street, and maybe the Museum of Modern Art, et cetera, again. Also, his furnace with a thermostat; rooms to play upstairs, downstairs; a real gas stove and fridge for regular meals. Electric lights instead of kerosene for homework. Wouldn't that be right for her and the kids?

"You know," Carol admitted to Press, "a sensible woman might consent to that, even prefer that. But sensible people don't run off to the woods and become Freaks. If the roof falls in, we'll be on your doorstep before you can say Jack Robinson." Rain was whispering in the trees, and a barred owl hooted coincidentally "Who Cooks For You, Who Cooks For You All."

"It'd be awfully cozy."

"I'll grant you it would," Carol assured him with unmistakable sympathy. "Could be best for us too, but I am what I am. Hippies are a kind of circle-jerk, you know," she confessed; he could hear her lips part in a smile.

"You're a beacon of honesty. I love you for it. It's why I want your company."

"But we're not caretakers," she pleaded, more seriously, as Press was starting another persuasive pitch, then stopped in mid-sentence. Capitalizing on his pause, she went on. "You know, I could have given you herpes but I didn't. I could have pleased you but made you sick," she stressed, though rubbed his arm soothingly. Press asked her what she thought of Chuck. Through her hand he felt her shrug.

"He's not an axe murderer, no."

"But beyond that?"

"I was with him."

Silence followed.

Chuck swung by en route to Maine again, but Press said no and then regretted it. He asked Melba if she thought Chuck was a loser. "Who isn't?" she laughed. Once, Al had done that run, before he switched to hauling cattle to the slaughterhouse. "Whatever floats your boat. I'm pretty hard up, bless the Good Lord."

"And you've got your marbles."

"You're damn right. Even us sluts who never knew where to get off."

Chuck left Press alone for a while as the weather chilled, until turning up he pitched a different proposal. "How about clearing out of cold storage before it's too late?" Down in Alabama where that old girlfriend lived, he knew a hotel to winter in. Not expensive like New Orleans and yet near a beach, and carny strippers liked to winter there. They wouldn't stand for any creep hitting on them—they got that all summer—a blind man like Press could be the perfect ticket.

He might leave Press there awhile, then pick him up.

"Why?"

"*Why?*—if you have to ask why, forget it! Or, remember you can always fly back."

Press threw caution to the winds. It seemed time to. "Tomorrow I'll know."

"Tomorrow you'll know? You need to print your last will and testament?"

Press laughed with him. "I just need to sleep on it. I always sleep on things."

"I'll write the girls. They'll like that. A blind guy, after a whole season of stripping for goggly chumps down the midway."

"Almost a mascot. My mouth is watering," Press said, though not believing a word of it.

Yes, he decided to pack. No pets to worry about. He wrote Melba a note to notify Dorothy and Darryl, not wanting to discuss what he was doing with either of them. As for Carol, the more fretting she might do the better.

"Ready to roll, baby, tomorrow," Chuck said. "All aboard for the nookie express!"

"Why me?" said Press.

"Company. And you got me out of a ticket. And I don't know where I'm going anyhow, and neither do you."

*A fool's errand,* Press's mind warned him mildly. Yet although he knew that Chuck might be an unreliable goofball in some ways, he wouldn't strip and dump him somewhere either. He'd drop him at an airport where his credit cards plus a kindly flight attendant or two could fly him back to Merrill Lynch-land or perhaps Melba-Carol-Dorothy territory. If blindness was a dead end ordinarily, why not live it up when a high flyer swung by?

The familiar rhythm of rubber on the road and shoulder against shoulder when the car swayed with the curves was tranquilizing. Did you have to understand life to plunge in? Even kindness, when he encountered it, was a riddle half the time. If you walked into a door and bloodied your nose, it was one thing, but empathy for handicaps had never been his thing when he himself had none. Empathy had been for people of good cheer. Yet Chuck in contrast of course was an operator, an improviser, not a betterment person. And improvising was the very essence of going blind, as the mind surfed continually through its library of memories for clues as to what was going on. When you were so easy to take advantage of, people generally didn't. A friend in need was a friend indeed, Press recited humorously. Not for most folks—when did you last help somebody in need?

Press unexpectedly remembered the boy who'd hung himself, and how little he had done to remedy the situation when Carol was telling him about the kid's antic behavior.

He had called his children before he left, and reminded himself to buy a butterfly book and a dinosaur book for Jeremy when he found a bookstore.

Molly had been excited because her rabbit had escaped and seemed to be having a ball outside, nibbling all the foliage.

Chuck had a tarp for the Great Smokies, where he wanted to camp for a night. Still had his temporary plates. He was amused that Press's wife had kicked him out for going blind, mentioned having met a man too rich for his wife to leave, so she simply would use a vibrator at night while lying in bed right beside him. Life was a mess, he said.

They purred along south, and not being able to see the congestion on the New Jersey Turnpike eliminated for Press the old irritations of travel.

Magic carpeting. The sky's shade of robin's-egg blue, then chartreuse darkened bluntly to black, with Chuck stopping only for bathroom calls, gas, and pizza and coffee.

"I'm in my element," he murmured. Somewhere in the Carolinas he propped up that tent fly for sleeping purposes. They lit a campfire and spread the gaggle of blankets, plus whatever unspoken trove of materials Chuck might be transporting and probably a gun to guard it with. He got a bit high but not obstreperously, chatted with himself without revealing secretive fodder for Press's musings. So far, as on the trip to Portland, he had no reason to regret throwing in his lot with Chuck.

Chuck left to use the phone booth several times and reflected rhetorically on whether he wanted to return to Ten Mile Farm next summer, speaking to Press in big-brother fashion, as if their age difference and sophistication were reversed.

Other campers made nesting sounds and irrational comments, or at cross-purposes, misheard each other, then apologized. Chuck's calls from the booth at the ranger's office were more complicated than he'd expected. Arguing with the other end—and employing the name Garth once again—he was apparently postponing a delivery, and needed more change from Press to feed the phone. He laughed and said, "They couldn't figure out where I am! Better than a hotel, that's for sure. No settled address is best."

He left to replenish their food, though Press, fingering ant hills on the ground, had no sure way of knowing that the car would return, just the tarp overhead. Like people's voices, he could recognize car engines, not by make or model but simply whose they were, and duly did hear Chuck's pull in next to him, with Cracker Jack popcorn, plus catfish gumbo, for a treat. "Good catfish, like Memphis. We may head to the Mississippi anyhoo. No ands, buts, or ors. I bet neither you or I ever thought we'd be doing this."

So, he wouldn't be rubbing sunscreen on the backs of a bunch of carnie strippers wintering by a pool. A fantasy, that. But Press's mind slipped into another. How about if Chuck soon dropped him off at the Amtrak station in Atlanta or some such place and he bought a roomette to Los Angeles. The porters would lead him to the dining car for every meal, the maître d' then seat him at a different table where he could strike up new conversations with obliging strangers, and in between mount to the bubble car where he'd really find acquaintanceships, as people helpfully described the landscape streaming by. Might even score a wife, in fact. Lonely widows and divorcees often took to a long rail ride, even in this airport age, and empathy was commonplace. An Amtrak read was not an airplane read and you'd board with different expectations. There's time for stories, for sympathy and friendship. Somebody might bring him home with her.

On the road after a sleep, he realized he didn't actually know which state they were in. Tennessee? The sun's position indicated they were traveling west. At lunch he was deposited in a restaurant with a margarita while Chuck placed more phone calls. Their matey relationship maintained its even keel, however, because Press was drifting willy-nilly in his wake. No money arguments, nor as to food or route. The scents in these restaurants, or outdoors, and eavesdropping on a hundred conversations unnoticed as just "the blind man"—there were rewards. He played it as it lay, enjoying the randomness of someone else's stop and go. Think of it as an amusement park, he told himself, where he was riding all the rides, and listening to yet another next-stool yak-yak at the candied-apple counter, the tapestry of America, while Chuck attended to business. The waitress wished him well and put her hand on his hand on his wallet in front of the other customers to take out the proper amount, tip included, then patted him as a signal to pocket it again.

"Where'd you get that funny name?" Chuck asked in the car.

"You mean Prescott?"

"Sure."

He pondered whether he wanted to be left off, as they pointed toward a declining sun and therefore the Mississippi. That Ozark commune Chuck had come from—did it still figure in his calculations? "What's the pot like they grow in Arkansas?"

"Well, they have their own trip there," Chuck said.

"So what's a trip like?"

"They never fed you any acid? Mescaline opens the heart. Acid's a rocket ride. Hash is like accelerated pot, even more euphoric. Coke's a great high. But do you know what we do with snitches? We tie them up and stick them in the bathtub and then turn on the water."

Press was taken aback. "So are you dropping me off in Little Rock?"

"Oh, I'm not going to Arkansas. I'm not certain where, but you can bail whenever you want. I have my principles." After a pause he added that Louisiana, for instance, was crawling with oil rig jobs for a pipe fitter. "I might go back to that. And they have rest homes there, if you like the climate."

"Nice idea." Was he afloat in the wrong place?

"The women are sweeter, Cajuns, Creoles."

"I like a drawl, so relaxed. 'Come back and see us. Don't be a stranger.'"

"The Bible Belt. They know about Noah's Ark. Two by two. Eating apples." Chuck laughed. "Some nook will fit you. Pay by the month and a damsel will come, make sure you're fed, and change your bed."

"You make it sound plausible."

"But isn't that what you already had, really?"

Having traded suppositions, they fell silent for some miles, except for burping from the driver's side. From his scent and a slight slurring, Press suspected he'd been drinking more than on their Portland drive. Uneasily he wondered not just whether Chuck was in the process of delivering drugs somewhere, but if perhaps he weren't also detouring right and left like this in order to snatch from the dealers whatever he had. A wildly dangerous proposition. Suddenly be a rich man.

Although they were on an interstate traveling at speed, the car teetered and shimmied. Press braced himself against the plastic dashboard or gripped the handle hanging above his passenger's-side door. Had he heard a paper bag crinkle as when somebody tipples slyly from a bottle? "Northwest, southwest? What do you do with a hundred thousand bucks?" Chuck chuckled. He said his father had been a rolling stone too, but a mean drunk, not agreeable. Liked to show up unexpectedly. "What could she do?" he ruminated. "Have him deported?" A friend of his mom's had got hitched to an immigrant who wasn't legal, and just called the Immigration Service when he turned ugly. Back to Latvia he went. As for child support, when Press broached the subject, Chuck's father's view had been that if a woman had a kid she ought to be able to support it.

"Like the hippies?" Press ventured, knowing that Chuck had one or two of his own stashed somewhere. Was it California, he hinted?

"Maybe kinda."

The dapple of sunlight with tree shadows flickered through the windshield. The car slithered but not at great speed. Their stops also seemed erratic or slipshod, shifting direction in relation to the sun. Had they left the interstate? Chuck's mind must be in turmoil, Press worried.

What happened that waning afternoon was that Chuck, rounding a mountain curve too fast, to his surprise lost control of the wheel or perhaps the car's dynamics, and hit a guardrail, then a tree. It was like the gargantuan thud in a balloon in a comic strip. Press was stunned, not cognizant of what had transpired for half a minute, except he felt in sequence his left knee, forehead, chest, and so forth. He discovered the seat belt had not broken and he was not perceptibly hurt, although aching. Half upside down, he wished he could see where they were or what had been done to the car, but couldn't. They were constricted by an accordioned car frame, wedged on its side, but Chuck cursed like a man in reasonably fair shape.

"Totaled! How are you?" He checked Press's head and leg with one hand. "Lucky, huh? We were both lucky." He could climb out through the windshield, he said, but told Press to relax and rest, picking broken glass off him. "They'll extract you, easy."

It sounded like Chuck was scrounging items from the back, and he retrieved the gun from the glove compartment. "Thank god the damned trunk popped open." A satchel or something bumped against the door frame. "Very lucky," he repeated, reminding himself that they hadn't been hurt, and collecting those temporary license plates, laughing mirthlessly because that too was good luck—a less traceable car.

"I think you're best staying where you are. Cops will be along and get you out. If you try it yourself, you'll get into trouble and fall. I'd appreciate it if mum's the word regarding me. Vermont, looking for a new life. A ride with a stranger. They'll put you on a plane for home. You've got nothing to answer for. We had a good time, don't you think, so don't feed 'em leads. You couldn't see what or wherefore anyhow."

Shortly he was gone, thrashing through the

brush up to the highway. "I'll call for help!" he yelled back. Soon, a car seemed to stop and pick Chuck up.

Thumbing for Arcadia? Press resolved to honor their palship by not mentioning Arkansas or communes or whatever. And he couldn't divulge the plate numbers or Chuck's last name because he didn't know either, and being blind, wouldn't know where they'd stayed. Songbirds in the trees close to the car began trilling normally again, as he groped carefully around for where the dashboard had buckled, how the steering wheel had missed impacting his chest and stomach, the crumpled door next to his ribs that wouldn't open when he tried it.

He was confident he would be rescued, and indeed after a while he was. A car stopped. People trundled down the slope. Without a need for the Jaws of Life his door was pried open, and an ambulance transported him for a checkup. Vermont's and Connecticut's police confirmed his identity, address, and blindish state. The vehicle, when hauled up to be scrapped, yielded no evidence of miscreant behavior beyond Chuck's telltale paper bag. Press told the detectives who questioned him that he had been on a joyride with an acquaintance named Chuck Something who was aiming for an oil rig job in the Gulf but had taken off after seeing that Press was okay.

"No fixed address, this drifter?"

"He said he had no wife. And no one he sent money to. Grew up in California. And he was trying the East."

"Kind of stupid to entrust your life to that kind of guy, don't you think? And he doesn't even want to collect his insurance?"

"Well, cheap insurance doesn't cover you, just the others. As far as 'stupid' is concerned, try being blind. And the old cliché is to walk in the moccasins of any man you're calling stupid."

The police in the room didn't respond.

"I'm blind as you can see. What else am I going to do?"

They kept him around for a couple of days before shipping him home to Melba.

# About the Author

Edward Hoagland (born December 21, 1932, in New York, New York) is an author best known for his nature and travel writing. His nonfiction has been widely praised by writers such as John Updike, who called him "the best essayist of my generation," and Joyce Carol Oates: "Our Chopin of the genre."

Hoagland joined the Ringling Bros. and Barnum & Bailey Circus in 1951 and sold a novel about this experience, *Cat Man*, before graduating from Harvard in 1954. After serving two years in the army, he published *The Circle Home*, a novel about the boxing world of New York. Soon after, he took the first of his nine trips to Alaska and British Columbia. During the 1970s he made the first two of his five trips to Africa. After receiving two Guggenheim Fellowships, he was elected to the American Academy of Arts and Letters in 1982. He is also a member of the American Academy of Arts and Sciences.

Mr. Hoagland has taught at The New School, Rutgers, Sarah Lawrence, CUNY, the University of Iowa, U.C. Davis, Columbia University, Beloit College, Brown, and Bennington, beginning in 1963 and retiring in 2005.

He divides his time between Martha's Vineyard and the Northeast Kingdom in Vermont.

**Center Point Large Print**
600 Brooks Road / PO Box 1
Thorndike, ME 04986-0001 USA

(207) 568-3717

US & Canada:
1 800 929-9108
www.centerpointlargeprint.com